**Amelia laughed. "Oh, please. Quit being melodramatic. You're acting as if we're star-crossed lovers."**

His hold on her arm eased, his fingers feeling more a caress than a restraint when he asked, "Aren't we?"

Nervous tremors crept up her spine. "No. We've barely even kissed."

Kisses she'd relived a hundred times, a thousand times, but still only the kiss the night of the rehearsal dinner and the kiss in her dorm room.

Amelia gulped, willing the memory to permanently vanish.

"Barely kissed?" He stared into her eyes for long moments, watching, waiting, then his gaze dropped to her mouth. "That's a problem easily remedied."

His head bent, but just as the heat of his breath touched her lips, burned her with more unforgettable memories, she turned her head.

"No." She couldn't do this. Wouldn't do this.

"Tell me I'm wrong, that you don't want me."

She wanted to, but couldn't lie to him. Couldn't lie to herself. Not a moment longer. She did want Cole. More than she'd ever wanted any man.

And it was wrong. Wrong. *Wrong.*

**Dear Reader**

Ever met someone and been fascinated by their life? That happened to me at the 2009 *RT Book Reviews* Booklovers' Convention. I met a fascinating lady who worked as a ship surgeon on an aircraft carrier and my muse jumped into warp-drive, creating the Stockton family.

The Stocktons are true-blue military, serving their country with honour and pride. How can loner Dr Cole Stanley *not* want to be a part of their tightly knit family? Unfortunately, he met the wrong Stockton daughter first, and didn't realise until almost too late. Now he's a man on an impossible mission: to win Amelia's love.

I hope you enjoy Cole and Amelia's story. I love to hear from readers. Please e-mail me at Janice@janicelynn.net, or visit me at www.janicelynn.net to find out my latest news.

*Janice*

# OFFICER, SURGEON... GENTLEMAN!

BY
JANICE LYNN

First published in Great Britain 2010
Large Print edition 2011
Harlequin Mills & Boon Limited,
Eton House, 18-24 Paradise Road,
Richmond, Surrey TW9 1SR



ISBN: 978 0 263 21731 5

Harlequin Mills & Boon policy is to use papers that are natural, renewable and recyclable products and made from wood grown in sustainable forests. The logging and manufacturing process conform to the legal environmental regulations of the country of origin.

Printed and bound in Great Britain
by CPI Antony Rowe, Chippenham, Wiltshire

**Janice Lynn** has a Masters in Nursing from Vanderbilt University, and works as a nurse practitioner in a family practice. She lives in the southern United States with her husband, their four children, their Jack Russell—appropriately named Trouble—and a lot of unnamed dust bunnies that have moved in since she started her writing career. To find out more about Janice and her writing, visit www.janicelynn.net

**Recent titles by the same author:**

DR DI ANGELO'S BABY BOMBSHELL
PLAYBOY SURGEON, TOP-NOTCH DAD
THE PLAYBOY DOCTOR CLAIMS HIS BRIDE
SURGEON BOSS, SURPRISE DAD

To Dr. Tamara Worlton Kindelan
for inspiring my muse by just being herself,
for her patience and generosity in answering my
questions. To Teresa Rose Owens for her
fabulous military knowledge.
And to Terri Garey, my wig-wearing,
fairy-winged partner in crime
(aka cover model-stalking *RT* roomie),
who believed I could and should write this story.
You rock, ladies!

Any and all mistakes regarding military life
are mine alone. Please forgive.

# CHAPTER ONE

WHAT was *he* doing here?

Dr Amelia Stockton's head spun at the sight of the uniformed naval officer crossing the sick bay of the USS *Benjamin Franklin.*

No way was Dr Cole Stanley really walking towards her.

And if that was Cole with the senior medical officer, well, she couldn't consider what his presence on board her ship implied, what that would mean to her hard-won peace of mind.

"Wow, Dr Stockton," Tracy whispered under her breath, nudging Amelia's arm. "Is that the new ship's surgeon? If so, sign me up for an elective procedure stat. Yum."

Amelia didn't turn to look at the petite blonde nurse, neither did she answer. She couldn't even if she wanted to. Along with her spinning head, now her throat had swelled shut.

*Cole really was on board her ship.*

She'd known the aircraft carrier's new surgeon would be arriving today. But Dr Evans's replacement was supposed to be Dr Gerald Lewis, not Cole Stanley, military surgeon and heartbreaker extraordinaire. Just because she hadn't seen him for two years, it didn't mean she hadn't instantly recognized that confident swagger, those piercing blue eyes, the crazy tune of her heart that had only ever played for him.

What was he doing here and why were her lungs crying for air?

From the overwhelming need to hit him for how he'd walked out on her and her family. That's why her head spun, her throat swelled, and she couldn't breathe. Her body functions hadn't gone haywire because of Cole himself, just what he'd done. Really.

Certainly, her fluttery heart had nothing to do with the last time she'd seen him, the things they'd said, done. Dear sweet heavens above, the last time she'd set eyes on Cole he'd kissed her until her lungs had felt just like they did this very moment.

"Dr Stanley, welcome aboard, sir." A corpsman saluted Cole, as did the physician's assistant, acknowledging Cole's higher military rank. "It's good to see you again."

"You, too, Richard. It's been a while."

He spoke with that voice. The one that haunted her sleep, her dreams. Nightmares, not dreams.

He shook both men's hands, said something about the naval hospital he and Richard had worked at together, but Amelia's ears roared, blocking out the details.

Cole. Was. On. Her. Ship.

No!

Oblivious to the turmoil he was creating in Amelia's safe, tight-knit world, in her mind and entire body—just as he'd always done—he acknowledged Tracy.

The nurse practically fell over herself batting her lashes and blushing up a storm. Puh-leeze. Tracy could do so much better. Any woman could. Sure, Cole came in an eye-catching package—and how!—but so did most poisonous snakes.

Cole Stanley was a low-down, belly-crawling snake of the worst kind. Yes, Amelia had once thought he'd hung the moon and walked on water, but her eyes had been opened.

Lastly, he turned to her, acknowledging her salute. He hesitated only the slightest of seconds, making her wonder if perhaps she'd been wrong, if perhaps he did know how his being there affected her, that perhaps he was equally as affected by seeing her after all this time.

"Dr Stockton." His gaze sought hers, searching, but for what she wasn't sure. Did he expect her to welcome him? Not after what he'd done to her, *to her sister*, surely?

Still, her heart sped up and stalled all at once when their gazes tangled for the first time in two years. Memories from the past assailed her. Memories of her and Cole, laughing, working, devouring pizza while he quizzed her, caring for patients together during residency. Memories of Clara, Cole and herself spending hour after hour together back during Cole and her sister's last year at medical school. They'd been two years ahead of her.

*Clara.*

Amelia sank her teeth into the soft flesh of her

lower lip, welcoming the pain, the metallic tang of blood.

A tentative smile cut dimples into Cole's cheeks. "It's been a while since our paths have crossed, too."

Not long enough. Not nearly long enough. *Oh, Cole, what are you doing here*?

His eyes were still bluer than the sea. His light brown hair still streaked with gold, as if the sun hadn't been able to resist reaching out and touching him. Clara had called him Dr Delicious. Amelia and Josie had agreed when they'd met Cole. After all was said and done, though, they'd dubbed him Dr Disastrous.

Cole was here. On board her ship. In the middle of the Pacific Ocean. Tainting her first real deployment.

Oh, yeah, Dr Disastrous fit and she suspected she was headed for the biggest disaster of her life. The *Titanic* of disasters. Especially since she wavered between wanting to punch his handsome face and…she wasn't sure what the other emotion battling for pole position was, but either way she didn't like the uneasy fluttering in her chest.

"You know him?" Tracy asked from beside her, nudging her again, much to Cole's obvious amusement. "You never said anything about knowing Dr Evans's replacement."

Taking a deep breath and reminding herself she was a lieutenant in the United States Navy, the middle daughter of Admiral John Stockton and a force to be reckoned with under any set of circumstances, Amelia shifted her gaze to her nurse.

"Dr Stanley graduated from Uniformed Services University of the Health Sciences with my oldest sister, Clara, two years ahead of me." She kept her face stoic, kept her tone even, emotionless. "With the last names so close, they were constantly thrown together and became acquainted. I met him during that time."

"Oh," Tracy said, her curious gaze going back and forth between them. "I see. Thrown together. Acquainted."

Cole's eyes flashed, hinting at the fire that burned beneath the surface, at the fact he'd known he'd be seeing her even if she hadn't known of his arrival.

"How is Clara?"

Despite the tight rein she always held on her emotions, Amelia's eyes narrowed. How could he ask that question? She wanted to scream, wanted to rip out his hair and kick him in the solar plexus. He'd been her big brother, her friend, her biggest crush, *her sister's fiancé.*

And then he'd walked away.

"She's fine." *Not really, but I'd never let you know how you hurt her, how you hurt me!* Oh, God, why was breathing so difficult? "She's serving as a flight surgeon with an air wing unit in the Middle East and has been commissioned there for about three months."

He studied her much as she scanned a blood smear beneath her microscope, looking at each individual cell, searching for anything outside the norm. "I'd heard that."

*Did you hear how she went a little crazy after you left her? How she volunteered for the most dangerous assignments? How I've wondered if I played a role in my sister's unhappiness and have had to live with that guilt?*

"Josie and Robert? Are they well?"

As if he really cared how her vivacious younger sister and daredevil brother were. Oh, please. Why was he making the conversation between them so personal when the crew watched? Did he know that if they were alone she'd give him a piece of her mind? That she'd tell him where he could go and she'd happily buy him a one-way ticket? Her family had taken him in as one of their own and all he'd left them with was fragmented relationships and hearts.

She despised Cole for what he'd done to her family.

Except that he was her superior officer and as such she had to pay him respect, whether she felt one iota of it or not.

Life could be so unfair.

"Robert is serving on board the USS *George Washington* as the senior medical officer and Josie is doing field training exercises at a combat support hospital. She earned her nursing degree. They're both fine. They're Stocktons."

His smile deepened at her last comment. It was a given all four Stockton children would succeed in life and medicine. Even when jerks like Cole came along and pulled the rug out from under their feet.

After her experience with Cole, Amelia had vowed never to give her heart to any man. Never did she want to feel the pain her devastated sister still hadn't recovered from.

Just look at how *much* she had been hurt, too, and she had simply had a hero-worship crush on Cole, not been in love with him. *Thank goodness.*

When a Stockton gave their heart, they gave it forever.

"I'm glad to hear they're doing well," Cole said, pulling Amelia back to the present, moving closer to where she and Tracy stood.

Although she couldn't possibly really smell him, she'd swear her nostrils filled with the musky scent of his skin, a scent once so familiar to her that, again, she was swamped by unwanted memories of when he'd starred in a daily role in her life.

"Your parents must be proud."

Amelia didn't answer. All four Stockton children had been raised to never show weakness to the enemy. Clara had put on a good front when Cole had dumped her, but privately her overachieving sister hadn't been able to "Suck it up and move on," as their father advised in any given situation. If she had, she'd have moved on, dated. Clara hadn't. There'd been no one since Cole. Amelia's heart ached at the enormity of her sister's pain, and her role in it. At her own pain. All at the mercy of this man's careless hand.

The others in the sick ward eyed them as if observing a ping-pong match. Cole's gaze bore into Amelia, waiting, but for what she didn't have a clue. For her to melt under his intense blue laser vision? For her to tense to the point she cracked into a thousand pieces?

Ha, he could wait until hell froze over.

She'd had enough.

"We've patients to see," she reminded the crew. "A full schedule this morning." She turned to the corpsman who eyed Cole with a bit of hero-worship. She recalled the look well. "Richard, since you and Dr Stanley are acquainted, why don't you show him the surgery suite? I'm sure it's similar to ones he's worked from in the past, but he'll want to familiarize himself with his new workstation and our equipment before getting started in the morning."

Cole's gaze lingered on her, but Amelia refused to meet his eyes again. Later, no doubt, they'd talk. Not that she wanted to talk to him. But how would they avoid doing so when they'd be forced to work together for the length of their deployment?

How would she deal with him at such close quarters? Although there were five thousand crew members aboard the aircraft carrier when the air wing was on board, she wouldn't be able to keep from interacting with Cole. Not in the medical ward.

What were the odds of being stuck in the middle of the Pacific Ocean with the last man on earth she'd ever wanted to see again?

And yet, even with that thought, she couldn't deny that she'd always known their paths would cross again.

How could it not when they'd left so much unfinished business between them?

* * *

Amelia Stockton in the flesh shamed Cole's memory of John Stockton's middle daughter. How had he forgotten how her melted-chocolate eyes sparkled with intelligence? How her high cheekbones accented her heart-shaped face? How her dark hair beckoned his fingers to free the upswept locks? How just being near her turned his insides outward?

No, he hadn't forgotten that. Neither had he forgotten how fiercely loyal the Stockton siblings were, how they'd been trained to be soldier tough from the time they'd worn diapers. Although Amelia's father had been civil when their paths had crossed recently, Cole suspected the majority of the Stocktons despised him.

All but Clara.

Then again, his former fiancée was the only one who knew the truth of what had transpired between them.

Cole stepped into the privacy of the surgical suite just off the sick ward, wondering if he'd really known what he was getting himself into when he'd finagled the assignment on board the USS *Benjamin Franklin*. He'd thought he had, but now, after seeing Amelia again, he had to wonder at his logic. Had he made a horrible miscalculation?

"I thought that went surprisingly well, considering."

He glanced at the corpsman serving as his guide. "Considering?"

Had word already gotten out? The military community, especially the military medical community, was small, but surely his and Clara's wedding fiasco hadn't been such a hot topic that two years later folks were still talking about it?

"Considering you obviously upset Dr Stockton in a former life."

"Obviously," Cole muttered, knowing exactly what he'd done that had upset the lovely Dr Stockton and wishing circumstances had been different, that their relationship hadn't taken the disastrous course it had. Tagging along with him and Clara, frequently working beside him during residency, she'd been like the kid sister he'd never had. Only, his feelings for his fiancée's little sister had developed into something much more intense than those of a big brother.

Something so intense that no matter how he'd tried fighting those feelings, how long he'd denied them, he'd had to face facts. He had been engaged to the wrong Stockton daughter. He'd wanted Amelia. Deep down, all-consuming, wanted her with a passion he'd never felt before or since.

"She's usually even-keeled," Richard continued, looking intrigued. He crossed his arms, leaning against the bulkhead. "I've never seen her lose her cool, or even come close as she almost did when you walked into the sick bay. Honestly, I didn't think anyone could rattle her infamous Stockton stoicism. What happened?"

"Between Dr Stockton and I? Nothing." Cole took in his shipmate's "yeah, right" expression and clarified. Better to get his version of the truth out before the rumor mill started something nasty that would add fire to Amelia's hatred toward him.

"I was engaged to her older sister. It didn't work out."

Didn't work out. Such an understatement, but what had happened between Clara and himself wasn't his secret to tell. He'd promised he'd never reveal that she'd been the one to call off their wedding. Yes, only because she'd beaten him to it, but she had spoken up before he had. She'd also sworn him to secrecy. Cole hadn't told a soul. Not even Amelia when he'd gone to her that night, desperately wanting to explain, to beg her to forgive him.

"You were engaged to Clara Stockton?" Richard whistled, looking impressed. "How come I never knew that?"

Cole shrugged.

"I met her, when I was inland. She was stationed nearby and joined several of us for drinks." He whistled again. "She's a looker."

"Yes," he agreed. Clara was a beautiful woman. On the day they'd met, she'd charmed him with her smile, her intelligence, her inherent toughness that was so in contradiction of her beauty-queen looks. She'd had a passion for medicine that matched his own and had professed to want the same things out of life. For the first time, he'd connected—really connected—with a woman.

For the first time, he'd felt a part of a family.

A wonderful, admirable family that would take on the world to protect each other.

Or to keep from disappointing each other.

Cole had longed for such a family his whole life. To be a part of something so strong.

He and Clara had studied together, worked together, laughed together. On the occasions they'd visited with her family, the Stocktons had welcomed him into their ranks with open arms. During their second year, asking her to marry him had seemed the logical thing to do. Becoming a real, permanent part of the Stockton family had seemed the most desirable thing he could imagine. He'd loved the time spent with them. With Clara. And Amelia.

Especially Amelia, he'd realized too late.

All the Stockton children were close, but Clara and Amelia shared a special bond, more best friends than sisters. Cole had spent as much if not more time with Amelia than he had Clara after Amelia had started medical school. Had gone from treating her as a kid sister to looking at her and seeing a woman who inspired fantasies.

"What happened?" Richard prompted when Cole stayed lost in his thoughts too long.

Cole inwardly sighed, but kept his shoulders square. He'd known coming aboard this ship would open old wounds. Wasn't that one of the reasons he'd come? To open those wounds so they could finally properly heal? "Clara and I realized we'd made a mistake in becoming engaged and broke things off. I've not seen her since."

Because Clara had completely changed her life plans and signed up to serve as a flight surgeon, going to helicopter flight school rather than a military hospital or aircraft carrier medical unit. They e-mailed on the rare occasion, but even that had grown further and further apart.

Richard's brows rose. "That would have been, what? Two? Three years ago?"

"Yes." Two long and torturous years where a single weekend had forever changed the course of his life. Two long and torturous years in which he'd tried to forget the Stocktons. Yet here he was, seeking out the Stockton he couldn't forget. He glanced around the surgical suite, taking in the neutral tones of the room. Dull gray bulkheads and metal cabinets of sturdy construction. "Tell me, where are the laparoscopic instruments? I'll put together a laparoscopic appendectomy set to my preferences. Then I want to go through and make sure the staples match the handles and check out the rest of the equipment so I don't run into any surprises mid-procedure."

Accurately sensing Cole's desire to change the subject, the corpsman explained the day-to-day basics in the surgical ward.

Not much different from what he'd expected, even better equipped than some of the sites he'd worked at prior to being deployed. Yet he couldn't recall his palms sweating and his heart racing at any other new assignment.

He knew the reason why.

The same reason he'd finagled his assignment on board this ship when doing so could cost him everything.

Amelia Stockton.

## CHAPTER TWO

LATER that morning, Amelia grimaced at the oozing wound on Corporal Wright's left inner thigh. "How long has the area looked like this?"

He shrugged his brawny shoulders. "Yesterday the spot was a little red. Today it looks like I got shot and the place festered all to hell."

The abscess looked nothing like a real gunshot wound, but she didn't bother explaining that to the eighteen-year-old. She hoped he never had reason to learn otherwise.

She turned to the cabinet that contained the appropriate supplies, pulled out a bottle of one percent Xylocaine, and drew up a syringe full of the numbing agent. "Are you allergic to any medicines?"

"I'm not allergic to anything." He shook his head, eyeing the syringe with pale-faced dread but trying not to show his dislike of needles. “What are you planning to do, Doc?”

“I’m going to open the area, drain the abscess, then pack the wound with special sterile packing gauze that will stay in the opened area for a few days.”

The corporal swallowed, his gaze lingering on the syringe. “Will it hurt?”

Amelia could laugh at the irony of his question. The men she dealt with had been through so much with their training, could endure great hardships, yet wave a needle and syringe in front of the biggest, baddest of the lot and he just might turn green in the face.

“Just a stick and some burn when the numbing agent is injected. After the medication, you shouldn’t feel a thing,” she explained.

She swabbed the area with an antiseptic solution then stuck the needle bevel up into the raised red area, numbing the overlying skin. Once she’d finished injecting the area, she dropped the used syringe into a sharps container then smiled at her still-pale patient.

“While the numbing agent is taking effect, my

nurse, Tracy, is going to set up a surgical tray so I can open the area and drain the abscess. I'll be back in a few minutes, and we'll get this taken care of."

Tossing her protective gloves into the appropriate waste receptacle, she left the small exam area and went into the room that served as the medical office.

Her gaze went to the computer on her desk and she winced.

Unless her sister was out in the field, she'd have an e-mail from Clara. She didn't want to tell her sister that her runaway groom was on board, that for the next few months Amelia would be working alongside him, spending more time with him than she'd like.

Than she'd like?

She didn't want to spend any time with Cole.

None. Never again.

If she'd never met the blasted man that would have been just fine.

Better than fine.

Her life would have been better. Less haunted by twinkling blue eyes and a sexily timbred voice that belonged to a man she'd once idolized. How could fate have been so cruel as to assign him to serve on the same ship?

"Need help?"

She spun, coming face-to-face with the source of her agitation. "Not from you."

His brow arched.

"Sir," she added, in deference to his higher rank.

Cole's gaze narrowed. "That's not what I was getting at."

"No? Not tossing around your weight, sir?"

"No." He said the word slowly, studying her.

Hello, she was not a bug under a magnifying glass and could he please just go jump overboard? Anything, just so long as she didn't have to look at him, didn't have to remember.

Her fingers clenched into tight fists. "Then what were you getting at, Dr Stanley?"

He crammed his hands into his pants pockets. "I suppose asking you to call me Cole would be useless?"

"You suppose correctly, sir."

Her eyes had to be tiny slits of disdain because

she was holding back none of her anger, none of her frustration. However, she desperately held back all of her hurt, all of the pain she'd felt at his sudden absence from her life two years ago when he'd been such an integral part of her very being for the majority of her university days. God, how she'd hurt, ached to her very core.

"Amelia."

"I did not give you permission to call me Amelia." She did not want to hear her name on his lips. Memories of another time, another place, of him whispering her name echoed through her mind, twisting her insides with feelings she'd denied for so long, feelings she didn't want. Not then. Certainly not now.

"Actually, you did," he reminded her, his gaze not leaving hers, pinning her beneath intense blue. "Just because time has passed, it doesn't mean I've forgotten."

That she understood. Two years certainly hadn't been enough time for her to forget a single thing about Cole. Sometimes she wondered if forever would be long enough or if she was doomed to spend eternity remembering every detail about the man looking so intently at her.

"We were friends once." The color of his eyes darkened to a deep blue. "Good friends."

Gritting her teeth, forcing her breathing to remain even, calm, she busied herself picking up a stack of papers from her desk and thumbing through them, reminding herself that she'd likely be thrown in the brig if she didn't get her emotions under control. How could he say that after...after...?

"Well, I have forgotten," she lied for pure self-preservation. "We were never friends. You're just some joker who had a laugh at my sister's and my expense and walked away from my family without a backward glance."

"Amelia," he began, then sighed, glanced over his shoulders down the narrow corridor leading off the sick ward to the office. When his gaze met hers next, steely determination had settled in. "We need to talk."

She crossed her arms, glared. He wasn't going to intimidate her if that's what he was trying to do. "Was the surgical suite not to your satisfaction?"

"I haven't been satisfied in years, Amelia."

"Call me Dr Stockton." She emphasized each word. "And I fail to see what your lack of satisfaction has to do with me."

"Don't you?" he asked softly, laughing with more than a hint of irony.

"Go away." She didn't look at him. She couldn't. How dared he bring *that* up, that crazy night, weeks after the non-wedding, when he'd come to see her and she'd eventually sent him packing? Besides, if he was trying to tell her he hadn't been with anyone for two years, she'd never believe him. Not in a million years. Which meant he was trying to play her for a fool. Again. She touched the desk, running her fingers over the smooth surface, collecting her wits before glancing up. "I never wanted to see you again."

"You made that obvious."

"Yet here you stand," she needlessly pointed out, riffling through papers as if she was bored with their conversation. Truth was, she needed to get away from him, needed to breathe. She couldn't breathe with Cole standing so close, with him eyeing her with such intensity.

"Unless orders come stating otherwise, I'm here for the full deployment. Dr Lewis has been assigned landside."

Six months. That was the usual duration of a surgeon on board a ship. Anything longer than that and their surgical skills might become rusty. Their usual days consisted of elective procedures such as vasectomies or ingrown toenail extractions, with the occasional gallbladder and appendix removal thrown in for good measure. Usually nothing as intense as working in a hospital setting like Cole must be used to.

"Good for you." She kept her tone level but, as she had for much of the day, inside she screamed. Loud and fierce and full of frustration.

Six months she was stuck working with him. Six whole months. Fine. She could do anything for six months. She was a Stockton.

"Which means we need to work through your anger for me."

She glanced up, met his gaze. "There's nothing to work through."

"You don't hate me?" He didn't look convinced. "Because I'm picking up pretty strong vibes that you'd like to dump me overboard."

He was picking up on that, was he? Good, maybe he'd take the hint.

"You don't rate that much of my thoughts." Liar, liar, pants on fire, but she couldn't admit that she'd thought of him often during the past two years.

Way too often.

"You've forgiven me?" He looked skeptical.

"For breaking my sister's heart and making a mockery of her the night before her wedding?" she asked, laughing cynically. *For making me look at you with stars in my eyes and breaking my heart right along with Clara's? Never.* "One thing you should know about us Stocktons, we're a loyal bunch. We look after our own and don't take kindly to anyone who messes with our family."

"I remember. You have an exceptional family." He smiled as if from fond memories. "Your father is one of the greatest men I've ever met."

"Yes, he is." No one was more dependable or

loyal than her father and Amelia loved him with her whole heart. He deserved her love because a finer man had never lived. John Stockton ruled with an iron fist and expected everyone to jump to his tune. Everyone did, all the Stockton children included. "He thinks you're a piece of no-good trash."

Cole flinched, but she felt no pleasure that her barb had hit home. She should be pleased, should want him to feel as much pain and remorse as humanly possible for the cruel way he'd treated her family.

Yet all she felt was the desire to be far away from him, to actually still be in her bunk, fast asleep, to wake up and find Cole's presence on board to be a horrible nightmare rather than her current reality.

Tiring of whatever game he played, she took a deep breath. "What is it you want, Dr Stanley?"

*You,* Cole thought, reeling at how forcefully the thought hit him.

He had always wanted Amelia.

For two years she'd haunted him, showing up in

his thoughts, featuring in his dreams. Knowing that at their last meeting she'd professed to hate him until the day he died, well, Cole had tried to forget her.

After all, even if she didn't hate his guts, it wasn't as if they could have a relationship. He'd been less than twenty-four hours from getting married to her sister and her family thought he was a heel.

Perhaps he was. Because when he'd watched Maid of Honor Amelia walk down the aisle during his wedding rehearsal, he'd wished he was marrying her, not Clara. For months, he'd tried to tell himself he was only have pre-wedding jitters, that he was being a fool, but when their eyes had met, his heart had gone into a mimicry of atrial fibrillation, fluttering like crazy and making him feel light-headed.

When the rehearsal had ended he'd gone outdoors, had had to have a moment to himself, to breathe, to process his thoughts, to figure out how he was going to tell Clara that he couldn't marry her, that he loved her, but not in the way he should, not with passion.

Amelia had followed him.

"Cole? Are you okay?"

He'd wanted to touch her. To pull her to him and let her heat warm him. He'd closed his eyes, fisted his fingers and nodded.

When he'd opened his eyes, she'd moved closer.

"Go back inside, Amelia."

But she hadn't. She'd lifted her hand, run her fingers across his cheek, slowly, tenderly. He'd trembled. Trembled like a schoolboy being touched by a goddess.

"Tell me what just happened," she'd prompted, her palm caressing his face.

Cole swallowed, reminding himself that he had to break things off with Clara, that as much as he wanted this moment, he couldn't grab it. Not until he'd told Clara the truth. That he couldn't marry her.

"We had the wedding rehearsal."

She studied him with those adorable chocolate eyes he loved to see dance with laughter. They weren't laughing now. No, they were staring up at him with great emotion shining in their depths. Emotion for him. "Are you having second thoughts about tomorrow, Cole?"

God, she was fearless, plunged ahead into dark waters without the slightest hesitation, knowing it was her God-given right as a Stockton to conquer the world.

"We shouldn't be having this conversation." *Not yet*.

"Why not?"

Had she moved closer or had he? Either way, mere millimeters separated their mouths. Her warm breath brushed his lips and need, hot and heavy, consumed him.

Need that he was tired of denying, tired of fighting.

"Because of this." He'd foolishly closed the minuscule distance, devoured her mouth with his, held on to her as if she were his only lifeline.

In that moment, she was the heat that warmed the cold numbness in his veins. Time had stopped and all that existed was the two of them.

Unfortunately, the moment ended all too quickly. Ended when Amelia pulled back, stared up at him with wonder and shock in her eyes. "Cole?"

"That shouldn't have happened." Not before he had the chance to break things off with Clara. "I need to talk to your sister."

He'd stepped back, determined to go find Clara, to put a stop to the events unfolding, then paused at the horrified look on Amelia's face.

"But, Cole, I..." She hesitated. "You..." Her fingers closed on his biceps, clamping down as if for support. "You can't, Cole. You kissed me. *Me*."

"Amelia." He raked his fingers through his hair, searching for the right words to tell her that somewhere along the line he'd fallen for her, but had denied his feelings even to himself for far too long. "This is complicated." Such an understatement. "Wait for me. Let me talk to Clara and wait for me."

Her lower lip disappeared into her mouth. "Are you getting married tomorrow, Cole? Tell me."

"No, I'm not getting married tomorrow." He'd tipped her chin toward him, pressed another kiss to her upturned lips. "Promise me that you'll wait. I'll explain everything."

Because he'd had to talk to Clara first, to put

a stop to their wedding, to be free to tell Amelia that it was her smile that warmed his soul.

Only, when he found Clara, she was crying, something he'd never seen her do. Never seen any Stockton do. He was hit with horrendous guilt, thinking she'd seen him and Amelia, had overheard what he'd said. She hadn't.

Instead, she'd had similar realizations to his own and didn't want to get married any more than he did. It seemed they'd both been hanging on to something that hadn't existed, something neither of them had wanted, but each hadn't wanted to hurt the other because they truly did love one another—just not in the way a man and woman should love the person they were going to marry.

He hadn't been able to refuse her one request, to leave immediately without explaining to anyone why they'd decided to call the wedding off. But that one request had cost him more than Clara could imagine.

"I'm busy," Amelia practically growled, making Cole refocus on the present, on the fact he stood on the USS *Benjamin Franklin* wanting to finish what he and Amelia had started years ago, wanting the fulfillment of the promises in her eyes when she'd looked at him that night. "So if there's something you want..."

He itched to reach out, to brush his fingers over her sleeked-back hair, to loosen the long silky strands from the tight bun at the base of her head. He wanted to know if she'd thought of him during the time since they'd last seen each other, if she remembered all the hours they'd spent together as friends, if she remembered the passion of their kisses.

"I want to put the past behind us." He couldn't have spoken truer words had he searched the Holy Scriptures.

"Fine, you want to put the past behind us." Her melted-chocolate eyes narrowed with growing irritation. "But why would I want to do that? Why would I even care?"

*Because not a day has gone by since I last saw you that you haven't crossed my mind.* For two years he'd waited, hoping she'd forgive him, hoping time would heal the rift, but she hadn't forgiven him and he'd gotten tired of waiting.

He'd done what he'd said he wouldn't do, what she'd asked him not to do before she'd kicked him out of her dorm. He'd come for her. This time, he wouldn't let her push him away. Not when there were unresolved feelings between them. One way or another, they would deal with the chemistry between them.

"We're going to be working closely together for the next few months, Amelia."

Her upper lip rose in an almost snarl at his use of her first name. He should call her Dr Stockton, but changing how he thought of her wasn't going to be easy.

"If we don't come to some sort of understanding, it'll affect our jobs," he told her honestly, knowing they did have to come to an understanding until they dealt with the past and appealing to her professionalism. "Neither of us wants that."

"You're the ship's surgeon. I'm the general medical officer. You stay in your surgical suite, and I'll stay in my sick ward." Her gaze burned into him, searing him with her hatred.

Hatred he deserved in her eyes.

"Our paths don't have to meet often," she

continued. "When they do, we'll pretend we don't see each other. No big deal."

He raked his fingers through his hair. He didn't want to pretend he didn't see her.

He wanted to see her. Lots of her. *All of her.*

Every delectable inch of her. Right here. Right now.

Wrong. He couldn't do that even if she begged him to. He couldn't kill his career. Sexual relations were strictly forbidden aboard ship and most often punished with a dishonorable discharge.

Hadn't he wanted time for him and Amelia to get to know each other outside the parameters of their former relationship? Hadn't he wanted time to win her trust before they acted on the physical chemistry? Wasn't that why he was here? He needed to focus on the here and now. On work. On building bridges with Amelia, not getting her into bed.

"I'll expect to consult with you on cases, *Dr Stockton.* I'll expect to help when the sick ward is busy, and I'm not in surgery. Don't be naïve in thinking we can easily avoid each other," he warned. "Our paths are going to meet often."

He'd see to it.

Her lips pursed in displeasure. "As I said, we'll just pretend not to see each other."

Frustration surged through him.

"No." Hell, no. Seeing Amelia was why he was here.

Her brow quirked upward. "No?"

"Under the senior medical officer, I'll be next in command in the medical division," he pointed out. "I won't have the GMO pretending not to see me. How would that look?"

"Who cares?"

"I care." Cole's comment stemmed from professionalism as much as personal desire.

"Afraid it might hurt your precious career?"

His career? Yes, suddenly he was afraid that being here, with her, might hurt his career. They needed forced time together, but just being near her again made reason fly out the door.

"I did mention that our not working as a cohesive team could hurt our careers," he reminded her. "Mine and yours. But I'm more afraid not working together will compromise our patients' health and the working environment of our colleagues."

True, but not the whole truth.

Her full lips compressed into a defensive bow. "I would never purposely compromise one of my patients or my crew."

"If you're unwilling to discuss cases with me because of the past, you might make the wrong choice regarding whether or not a person needs a surgical consult."

"Were you not listening? I just said that I wouldn't compromise my patients' health. If a patient needs a surgical consult, I'll send him or her to you." Her gaze narrowed, nonverbally telling him where he could go and that she'd love to shove him down the elevator shaft to take him there. "Got it?"

"Amelia—" At her glare, he sighed. "Dr Stockton," he began again, wishing he knew what to say to mend the bridges he'd had to burn. He hadn't had a choice.

"For whatever it's worth." He kept his voice steady, held her gaze even though looking away would have been easier than seeing the contempt burning in her brown eyes. "I'm sorry about what happened with Clara. I never meant to hurt her."

Amelia's pupils dilated and she failed to hide the pain that flashed across her face.

Pain that he'd caused.

Almost immediately a frigid glare replaced her hurt.

"And what you did to me?" she asked, studying him with eyes he wanted nothing more than to lose himself in. She would likely never forgive him, never let her guard down. "Are you sorry for that, too, Dr Stanley?"

"More than I can say."

Maybe, just maybe, a six-month stint with her would give him the chance to put right a few wrongs from his past.

# CHAPTER THREE

"Wow, you're really working up a sweat today," Suzie, one of the two on board dentists and Amelia's bunk mate, commented when she climbed onto the elliptical machine next to Amelia.

"You've no idea," she mumbled, knowing she'd already beaten her best time on the exercise equipment by several minutes, yet still she pushed on. Faster and faster, drops of moisture running down her face, between her breasts, causing her sports bra to stick to her like a damp second skin.

Truth was, even if she weren't on a stationary machine, all her efforts would be for naught.

Some things couldn't be run away from.

Like Cole.

From the time she could walk, Amelia had faced life head-on. With one exception. Cole. Until the night before her sister's wedding. As the maid of honor, she'd walked up the aisle toward him and been filled with longing. Longing she'd had no right to feel. Longing that had almost stopped her in mid-step.

She'd always been a bit in love with her sister's perfect fiancé, had always hoped to meet a man like Cole someday. But during the rehearsal, when their eyes had met, she'd seen something she'd only caught glimmers of previously.

She'd seen matching attraction. Cole had wanted her. And not in a way a soon-to-be married man should want another woman, especially his bride-to-be's little sister. He'd looked at her the way some dark, secret, forbidden part of her had always wanted him to look at her. He'd looked at her as if she were the most desirable woman in the world and he couldn't believe he was lucky enough to stand in her presence, to see her walking down the aisle toward him.

Which was ridiculous.

She wasn't his bride-to-be, wasn't desirable. But even now she could recall the way he'd stared at her, and the way her heart had pounded in response to his burning blue gaze.

"Um, Amelia." Suzie interrupted her thoughts. "You want to talk about whatever's eating you before that machine starts smoking?"

Amelia slowed her pace a few notches, dragged air into her protesting lungs and shrugged. Her bunk mate would prise the truth out of her eventually. By being up-front, perhaps she'd waylay her friend's naturally suspicious nature and avoid questions she didn't have answers to. "My sister's ex-fiancé is the new surgeon. I don't like him."

Two simple sentences that held a world of complexity and heartache.

Suzie programmed her stair machine to her preferred workout routine. "Ouch. That sucks." Her gaze flickered past Amelia to the workout area entrance. "Is he really, really drop-dead gorgeous?"

Amelia glared. "What do you mean, is he drop-dead gorgeous? What does it matter what he looks like? He's a creep who broke my sister's heart."

*Who broke my heart.*

"Never mind. He is or you'd have said so." Her friend's lips curled into a smile that flashed pearly whites that would make all her dental professors proud, her gaze still focused beyond Amelia toward the entranceway. “Besides, I see for myself, and I agree. He is really, really drop-dead gorgeous. Amazing eyes and that body—oh, my. Somebody should slap a warning label on that man’s forehead because just looking at him may send me into cardiac arrest.”

Amelia battled to keep from looking toward the door. Cole was there? In the workout room? Why? Well, she knew why. A man didn’t have a body like his without being active.

“I might not have guessed it was him except he’s new. No way would I not have noticed if Tall, Dark and Yummy had ever been in this room before.” Suzie gave a smug smile, gliding back and forth on her elliptical machine with practiced ease. “Plus, he walked in, scanned the room and paused when his gaze settled on my very own Little Miss Sunshine.”

Cole was looking at her? Why? Ready for round two? Or was it three? Please don’t let him be looking, because even after two years and a million attempts to compartmentalize what had happened between them, she still felt ill prepared on how to deal with Cole. Was he still looking? She was not going to check. She wasn't. She didn't even want to.

Much.

And then only to glare.

"He's still looking, by the way." Suzie's voice held a teasing quality. "Just in case you were wondering."

The heat spreading across her cheeks had nothing to do with her friend's knowing snicker. Overdoing it on the elliptical was why her face burned. Really.

"Don't stare," she ordered in the sternest tone she could manage, trying to keep her pace on the stair machine casual rather than returning to her frantic break-neck speed on a new wave of adrenaline. Why the heck had she pushed herself to the point her limbs were water? To the point her black gym clothes clung to her body? To the point her face was on fire? "He might think we're talking about him."

"Honey," Suzie said, her eyes still eating Cole up, "he's used to women talking about him. Has to be. That is one fine specimen of man. Looking at him makes my tongue want to wag and I'm not ashamed to say so."

"Hello. The man broke my sister's heart into a billion pieces," Amelia reminded her, not mentioning her own billion-pieced heart.

Suzie's gaze reluctantly returned to Amelia. "What happened? Give me the gory details so I can look beyond his lip-smacking exterior to the disgusting bastard filling."

The gory details? That might be a bit of a problem. Amelia didn't know the specifics. Even in the midst of a crying jag, Clara hadn't offered the whole story. Afraid of what her sister might say as to the reasons Cole had called off the wedding, Amelia hadn't pushed for the full details.

"They were engaged to be married. Following their rehearsal, he decided he didn't want to be married after all and left." How could her words sound so calm? So just stating the facts? She was talking about an event that had forever changed her sister's life. He'd made Clara weak. Her, too. "Clara was devastated."

Amelia had been, too. And guilty. Had her questioning him on the way he'd looked at her when she'd walked up the aisle, their amazing kiss that shouldn't have happened, played a role in Cole calling off his wedding? Of course it had. She'd unwittingly sabotaged her sister's happiness. Oh, yeah, she'd lived with guilt.

"I see why." As if she couldn't resist, Suzie's eyes shifted toward where Cole warmed up by stretching his long limbs.

Amelia's traitorous gaze played follow the leader to Cole, not content to only see him in her peripheral vision.

He wore gray cotton gym shorts that loosely hung to mid-thigh, riding up to reveal well-defined quads when he touched the tips of his tennis shoes. A white cotton T-shirt with "NAVY" emblazoned across the front caressed his thick chest. He straightened, reached high over his head, his shirt hem riding up to reveal a sliver of toned abdomen.

Suzie sighed with great appreciation. "If I'd thought I was going to spend the rest of my life curled up in bed next to that and suddenly found out I wasn't, I'd be devastated, too."

"Be serious," Amelia snapped, wanting to

physically drag her friend's eyeballs away from Cole, practically having to do the same to keep her own gaze from bouncing around like an over-eager puppy wanting another glimpse of tanned flesh. Did he know they were talking about him? "There's more to a man than the way he looks."

"Yeah, but when a man looks like he does, a girl can forgive a lot of flaws." Suzie sighed, moving her arms back and forth in motion with the handlebars, her workout making her sound slightly breathless.

Or maybe it was Cole making her friend breathless.

"I can't forgive his flaws." Amelia refused to be so superficial. She'd once been fooled by his in-your-face male magnetism and charm. Never again would a man weaken her that way.

"Yeah." Her friend nodded in agreement. "But you're made of fortified Stockton steel and only have an Achilles' heel for stray kittens."

"Stray kittens?" Amelia scowled. "I do not."

"Sure, you don't," Suzie teased, knowing Amelia well enough, unfortunately, to push her buttons. "If you lived inland you'd have a yard full of fuzz-balls, and you know it."

Would she? Amelia rarely thought of what her life would be like if she weren't in the military. Not that she'd ever considered doing anything other than military medicine. She hadn't. It's what their family did. Her father had been a surgeon with the navy, her mother an air force nurse.

"I don't even like cats," she protested half under her breath. She'd actually never had a pet to know if she'd like a cat or not. Growing up in a military family where they'd lived either on base or with whatever relative could look after them while their parents served their country, they'd moved too often to accumulate pets. Or close friends. Was that why she'd latched onto Cole? Had treasured their friendship so much?

"Don't look now, but something else you don't like is headed this way." Suzie slid a sly look her way. "Or should I say someone?"

Before she could stop, Amelia glanced toward where Cole had been stretching. Her gaze collided with his vivid blue eyes. His lips curved upward in an amiable, hopeful smile and her breath caught in a way no exercise equipment could ever induce.

In a way that was pure Cole Stanley breathless.

She almost agreed with Suzie. A woman could forgive a multitude of sins when a man looked like Cole. It would be easy to get caught in his charm, in the warmth of his smile, the intensity of his azure eyes, the lure of his friendly demeanor. He wasn't her friend, though.

In that moment, Amelia hated Cole. Hated him for hurting her family, hated him for whatever it was that seeing him did to her insides, hated him for turning her brain to mush by merely slanting his gorgeous mouth upwards.

She ignored the little voice warning that she protested too much, that hate was a strong emotion and she should be careful: the opposite of hate was love.

That was one emotion she could never feel for Cole.

Great. Cole sighed in frustration at Amelia's narrow-eyed rejection of his smiled peace offering. Right back to square one.

For just a millisecond when their gazes had met, before the anger had slid into place, he'd glimpsed the same curiosity that burned in his soul. A curiosity that made him long to open Pandora's box and dive into the unknown depths of whatever mysteries lay between them.

He cursed that her anger had quickly bubbled to the surface and drowned out all other emotions. Amelia hated him for what she believed he'd done to Clara and she wasn't going to forgive him any time soon. If ever.

Damn it. He wanted her forgiveness. Now. Yesterday. *Two years ago.*

Patience had never been one of his virtues, but surely he didn't expect her to welcome him on his first day aboard ship?

No, Amelia Stockton was like a wild mustang. To gain her trust would require endurance, fortitude, strength of mind, diligence.

Why Amelia? Why Clara's sister? He'd asked himself why a thousand times. More. But he never came up with a satisfying answer.

Satisfying. A wry smile twitched at his lips. He

hadn't lied when he'd told Amelia he hadn't been satisfied in years.

He hadn't. Amelia had bewitched him and he simply didn't want anyone other than her. No doubt that played into his current level of frustration, but sex for the sake of sex had been a poor substitute. After a few failed attempts to forget Amelia, he hadn't been willing to settle for that.

He still wasn't, which explained the insanity of his request to serve on the USS *Benjamin Franklin*.

Amelia's glossy dark hair was swept back in a ponytail, swishing to and fro with each movement of her tight body. Her legs pumped the elliptical machine back and forth, her arms making a rapid ski motion while she stared straight ahead as if she couldn't see him, as if he no longer existed. Was that what she'd done? Written him out of her life as if they'd never shared kisses that had set his insides aflame?

Cole bit back an appreciative groan. He wasn't the type who ogled women at the gym. Usually. Today, he was thankful his gym shorts were loose.

Otherwise he'd find himself in an embarrassing predicament. She was hot—and not just because sweat glistened on her skin, dampened her hair.

He wanted to step into her fire and go up in smoke. Rich, deep, *satisfied* smoke.

"Ame—Dr Stockton," he recalled just in time, climbing onto the elliptical on the opposite side of her, reminding himself to take baby steps, not to push too much too soon or his hopes for the future would be what went up in smoke.

Without glancing toward him, a scowl was her only response.

Cole reminded himself not to jump the gun. Eventually, Amelia would come around, would see that he was the same old Cole who had once been such an integral part of her life. He hoped. He desperately wanted that position back. But this time he didn't want her to see him as her sister's fiancé and he sure didn't want her feeling like his baby sister.

Not that he believed she'd kissed him that way. No, Amelia had wanted him the way a woman wanted a man when the chemistry is crackling.

They'd crackled.

"Hi," a pretty Asian woman on Amelia's right called, leaning forward. "Amelia was just telling me you're the new surgeon." The woman ignored the I'm-going-to-kill-you glare coming her way from Amelia and gave him a welcoming nod without missing a beat on her machine. "I'm Suzie Long, one of the two dentists. Welcome aboard."

Grateful for a friendly face in enemy territory, he flashed a smile. "Nice to meet you, Suzie. Or should I say Dr Long?"

Blowing out an exasperated huff, Amelia muttered something unintelligible under her breath.

"Unless I'm telling you to open wide," the petite woman flirted, giving him a friendly smile, "it's Suzie."

Liking her, Cole laughed. "I'll keep that in mind."

In between them, Amelia stopped exercising, waited for inertia to catch up with her machine. The moment the movement stilled enough for safe dismount, she climbed off. Without a word to him and only a glare at the woman she'd been chatting with until he'd joined them, she walked off. Picking up a gym bag, she took out a sports bottle and took a long drink.

Cole tried not to watch. But he did. When it came to Amelia he couldn't help but watch. His throat grew dry, withering him with thirst. A thirst he desperately wanted to quench, but which only her lips could quell.

Medical school had trained him to do without sleep. The navy had trained him to do without basic life necessities. Neither had prepared him for denying his need for Amelia.

"You're so barking up the wrong tree," the dentist advised, following his gaze to where Amelia tightened the lid and dropped the water bottle back into her bag. "Not meaning to be blunt, but she can't stand you."

"I know." He sighed. "She has reason."

"She told me."

Cole cut his gaze to her. "She told you?"

"About her sister and you? Yep."

That surprised him.

Apparently reading his mind, the woman went on. "I doubt she's told anyone else you were a runaway groom, though. Shame on you for that, by the way!" Her smile softened her reprimand. "Amelia and I are bunk mates."

Runaway groom? He cringed at the description. Yes, he supposed that's how Amelia saw him. He glanced toward the woman two machines down. "You're Amelia's bunk mate? That's good to know."

Her expression was positively wicked. "In case you ever want to visit?"

"In case I ever want to visit," he repeated, his gaze going back to where Amelia lifted a dumbbell from its rack. Her toned flesh flexed as she extended the weight, muscles shifting temptingly with her movements, making Cole think of other ways her muscles would shift with movement.

Snorting, Suzie's gaze followed his. "Yeah, right. She would have you court-martialed if you so much as made a pass at her. Even if she didn't think you were the scum stuck to the bottom of the boat, she wouldn't be interested in an on board romance. Her career means too much to her for that."

Not that on board sexual activities didn't occur, but one could lose everything if caught. Much better to take their time aboard ship to reestablish their friendship and earn her trust, as planned. Not destroy his career as well.

Besides, the only reason his request to serve aboard Amelia's ship had been granted was that they both valued their careers enough not to put them as risk. Of that, he had no doubt. When they were at port call, off ship, well, all was fair in lust and war, but Cole hadn't pointed that out.

Suzie eyed him expectantly, waiting for his comeback, waiting for him to tell her what she wanted to know. What she already knew because she could see his interest in Amelia as plain as the nose on his face.

If he played his cards right, she might just be on his side. An ally behind enemy lines. Something he hadn't counted on. Not beyond the person who'd helped him get on board.

A slow smile spread across his face. "What I want to know is whether or not you think I'm the scum on the bottom of the boat, too?"

Obviously pleased by his response, the woman laughed. "I think you're far worse than the scum on the bottom of the boat, but I'm pretty sure I'm going to like you, anyway."

His gaze went back again to where Amelia curled a free weight, her muscles flexing beneath her sleek skin.

"At least that'll be one person in your room who likes me."

But if the way Amelia kept casting surreptitious glances toward him was anything to go on, she felt the chemistry between them that hadn't let up with time and distance.

He understood she was confused. Understood her dislike of him. Understood she was going to combat the underlying attraction between them.

Cole was ready for the fight of his lifetime and when all was said and done, he'd win Amelia's forgiveness.

The stakes were too high not to win.

# CHAPTER FOUR

COLE had been on board the USS *Benjamin Franklin* for two weeks and had fallen into a routine. He scheduled procedures early morning, finished in the surgery suite on most days by ten, and then hung out in the sick ward "helping" until all patients had been examined.

Amelia could do without his kind of help.

His kind of help distracted her.

Made her feel as if she were in need of a doctor herself.

Tachycardia, shortness of breath, dizziness, flushing, mental cloudiness, thick tongue, tingling breasts.

Pathetic. Absolutely pathetic that he was having such an effect on her body. Her breasts did not tingle. It was more like an itch. And not the kind she needed scratched. At least, not that kind of scratching. No, it was more the allergic-to-jerks, stay-away-from-me type of itch. A reaction one had when something was harmful to their health. *Yeah, right.*

"I heard Dr Carter—" the other medical doctor on board "—wasn't feeling well and you're by yourself. Need my help?"

Think of the devil and there he was, looking way too handsome in his scrubs. His stethoscope dangled around his neck and he looked the picture of good health. Not like he'd barely slept for the past two weeks because of a disturbing presence from his past. Irritated that she was the one looking like the walking dead, she gritted her teeth.

"No." What she needed was him off her ship so she could get back to her regularly scheduled life program.

"Fine." His smile never faltered.

No matter how many times she cut him off, he just kept smiling, kept being nice, kept coming back for more. He was driving her crazy, making her remember too many of the reasons she'd fallen under his spell to begin with.

"I'll see who's in triage and take care of whoever I can."

During his short time on board, Cole had gained the respect of the medical crew by jumping in to help wherever needed. He triaged patients, took blood pressures, gave shots, whatever.

Not only had he gained the crew's respect, he'd gained their friendship. Everyone liked him. Except Amelia.

"Hey, Dr Stockton, is it okay if Dr Stanley uses bay two? He's going to repack an abscess."

Cole stepped back into the sick bay, holding a triage sheet. Having heard Richard's question, he glanced at her, seemingly waiting for her approval. As if what she said made any difference whatsoever. Along with Richard and the rest of the crew, the senior medical officer thought Cole was the greatest thing since butter on toast.

Amelia had thought the same once upon a time. During medical school she'd idolized him, had viewed Cole as the perfect man. Funny, generous, intelligent, handsome, charming, compassionate. Had she not loved Clara so much she might have resented her sister's perfect life. Beautiful inside and out, Clara had held Cole's heart from nearly the moment they'd met. Only, in the end, Cole had kissed Amelia and walked away from both women.

"If that's okay?" he added to the corporal's request.

"Fine." She turned away, knowing she was unnecessarily brusque yet unable to bring herself to show any grace. If she gave Cole an inch, he'd take a foot. She had to keep her distance for her own peace of mind, from loyalty to her sister.

Clara, whom she hadn't been able to tell that Cole was on her ship despite their e-mails. Clara, who had volunteered for yet another crazy assignment. Clara, whose notes sounded so unlike the woman she'd once been while engaged to Cole.

Oh! She despised what he'd done to her big sister and she clung to that like a drowning woman clutching a life preserver.

"There's a positive strep throat in bay one," Tracy said, snagging Amelia's thoughts back to where she was washing her hands.

She'd scrubbed so hard she was surprised to still see skin.

Drying her hands, she nodded at the nurse. "Thanks."

Tracy's face twisted in thought then she pulled Amelia aside. Under her breath, she quickly spoke. "I wouldn't say this if I wasn't your friend, but the whole crew has picked up on your...not *hostility* but a definite lack of friendliness toward Dr Stanley."

"And?" Amelia fought to keep her face emotionless. As she'd told Cole on that first day, she wouldn't let her animosity toward him interfere with the care of her patients. In her mind, she'd stuck to that. She may not like him, but she was doing her best to be professional. She'd even set up several patients to see him during his stint thus far. Obviously, however, she hadn't done such a great job of hiding her feelings from the crew, which truly did affect both their jobs.

Tracy looked uncertain about going on. "You're one of the fairest people I know, Amelia. Always level-headed and logical. Kind, too. Yet, with Cole, you're...prickly."

"Prickly?" She wanted to laugh. "Prickly" was as good a word as any to define how she felt about being forced to work with Cole. Just call her Cactus Woman. "It's true I do my best to avoid the man, but I am professional when our paths cross." Usually. "He's the one who keeps invading my workspace." And her workout space, her dining hall space, her dreams.

"Invading your space?" Tracy frowned, and chided gently, "You're lucky he's such a caring doctor. Not all would spend their free time seeing more patients so he can lighten someone else's workload. Maybe you should give the guy a break."

Okay, Tracy had a point. Cole did go above and beyond his workload and try to make the sick ward run more smoothly. He was an excellent, caring doctor. And, no, she really hadn't rolled out the welcome mat, but surely no one thought she should? As gossip always did, word had gotten out.

"All I ask is that he stay out of my personal space, take care of his patients, allow me to take care of my patients, and beyond that, it's really irrelevant if I like him. Every crew member doesn't have to like every other crew member. Actually, to expect that is idyllic and naïve," Amelia pointed out, knowing she was being too defensive. "He isn't someone I can like because of the past, but I can tolerate him for the time we serve on board together."

"So he used to be engaged to your sister? So what?" Tracy shrugged in frustration. "If he didn't love her, he did her a favor by ending things before the wedding."

Anger bubbled deep in Amelia's belly. "A favor? You think he did my sister a favor by breaking their engagement?" she fumed, clenching and unclenching her hands at her sides.

She wanted to scream that he'd waited until the night before their wedding to bestow his *favor*. That her family had arranged to all be home, that their friends had all been there, that Clara had been left to tell everyone the wedding was off because, after getting cold feet, he'd left. Left! Deserting Clara to face the music alone. Deserting *her*, letting her wait hopelessly for him, telling her by his actions all she'd needed to know, leaving her with mountains of guilt.

As much as she'd like to point out what a cad

Cole really was, Amelia couldn't bear to make Clara's humiliation public. Nor her own, particularly not in the medical ward where she might be overheard by other crew members and perhaps even Cole.

"See, this is what I mean. Look at you. Your face is red, your voice is low, and your words are erupting from between gritted teeth." Tracy gave her a concerned look. "Before Dr Stanley arrived, we all thought you were one cool cookie and great to work with. Now…"

Now they all thought she'd turned into a witch.

One with pointed shoes and a wart on her nose.

Maybe she had. Cole obviously brought out the worst in her.

She'd had enough.

"Well, if you'll hand me my broom, I'll fly on over and see the strep throat in bay one."

"Amelia." Tracy clutched her shirtsleeve. "Please think about what I said. Whatever happened between Dr Stanley and your sister is in the past. Maybe he did make mistakes but whatever happened, he's a great guy now and genuinely seems to want your forgiveness. Let the past go."

Let the past go.

As if it was that simple.

As if it weren't her right as next of kin to nail the jerk who'd hurt and humiliated her family, and crushed her heart.

As if it wasn't in her best interest now to protect that heart at all costs by keeping distance between herself and Cole.

The object of her animosity stepped out of bay two, peeled off a pair of disposable gloves and dropped them into a waste receptacle.

He glanced up, met her gaze with his cerulean one and gave her a smile. The same smile he flashed every chance he got, regardless of who saw. One that said, *Forgive me*. One that said, *I'm sorry*. One that said, *Remember me. The me you adored. The me you kissed as if we were long-lost lovers*. One that said he hadn't forgotten two years ago, and he wanted her still.

Maybe that was why she couldn't forgive him.

Maybe that was why she clung to her anger so fiercely.

Because if she quit hating Cole for what he'd done to Clara, to her, if she forgave him, she'd have to confront what she saw in his eyes.

Cole wanted her.

A fact that left her uncomfortable in her own skin.

Worse, if she stopped clinging to her anger at Cole, she'd have to face her own feelings—what she'd been feeling when their gazes had met and how her world had stood still during a wedding rehearsal meant to forever link him to another woman.

But if those were her reasons for disliking Cole, what did that say about her? That she was a coward? Not worthy of the crew's respect?

Amelia was no coward.

After all, she was a Stockton.

She turned back to her nurse. "You know, Tracy, I owe you and everyone an apology. I have been walking around with a chip on my shoulder where Dr Stanley is concerned. If that has affected my job performance or my interaction with the crew, I'm sorry."

Looking relieved, Tracy smiled. “It’s okay, Amelia. We were just a bit worried as it’s so unlike you.” Tracy gave her a kind look. “Does your sister have any idea of how loyal you are? How lucky she is to have you for a sister?”

Loyal? Amelia didn’t feel loyal. She felt like a traitor. She had betrayed her sister in the worst possible way.

That was why Cole had contacted her after the breakup. Why he’d come to see her that night a few weeks later. After he’d stood her up! Wait for me, he’d said, and then he’d left. Without a word. Had he really thought she’d talk to him? Had he really thought she’d just let him move from one Stockton sister to the next without batting an eyelash of protest at him showing up on her doorstep, saying he couldn’t get her out of his mind and wanted a relationship with her?

He wanted a relationship with her now.

He hadn’t spoken the words out loud, but when he looked at her, the message blazed in his eyes.

But whatever chance they’d had disappeared the moment he’d left her waiting, the moment he'd walked away and left Clara to deal with everything on her own. Maybe, under the circumstances, they'd never even had a real chance.

Still, regardless of what Cole wanted or even what she wanted, she had a job to do, a responsibility to her crew, and Amelia took her responsibilities seriously.

"You're right. It is time I let the past go." She intentionally said the words loud enough for the others to hear.

Cole's eyes widened, then narrowed.

She arched a brow in challenge at him, a slow smile curving her lips. Somehow his distrust made swallowing her pride, facing her fears where he was concerned, a little easier. She'd do what was right for her crew, what they needed to see from her for the overall good.

As her father would say, sometimes a man—or woman—had to prove their worth by taking one for the team.

For the next few months, Amelia would take one for the team and pray she didn't live to regret her decision.

* * *

A bad feeling crawled up Cole's neck. One of those that warned something wasn't right.

Amelia walked toward him. Of her own free will. No gun to head necessary.

"How did Corporal Wright's abscess look? Healing well?"

Had she really just spoken to him of her own accord? Smiled at him with her mega-wattage smile?

Something was definitely off-kilter.

Besides his equilibrium.

But who was he to look a gift horse in the mouth? Amelia was talking to him, smiling at him. The feeling was too good for him to do anything other than bask in her attention for however long the aberration lasted.

"The wound is draining more than the area should be with as much time as has passed." Had his voice croaked? "I want another culture to see if he's developed a secondary infection."

Her smile didn't miss a beat, perhaps even kicked up another few watts. "Any new symptoms?"

A stun gun blasted him, scrambling his thoughts. He forced himself to focus on his patient, on science, on anything but how Amelia's smile re-routed his circuitry.

"Increased redness and drainage. Nothing else."

"Good." She stared expectantly at him.

Cole had a flashback to a stolen moment between patients in the busy E.R. where they'd both been pulling residency hours. She'd looked tired, he'd cornered her, teased her, and she'd looked up at him with expectancy. And longing.

How had he missed that look at the time? How had he not realized what had been happening between them? Because he'd definitely felt longing in return. Only he'd stuck a big fat brotherly label on everything to do with Amelia so he hadn't had to feel guilty at how his feelings for her had been growing.

"I haven't re-dressed the wound yet." Why did his tongue feel like a lead weight? "Do you want to look prior to seeing your next patient?"

"Thanks. I'd love to." With another smile, she nodded, as if she'd been waiting for the invitation. Just as she'd done when he'd been with a patient and she'd wanted to observe, only this time his head spun.

Maybe while she was in such an agreeable mood he should suggest a private talk in the office. One where he pushed her up against the wall and kissed her until they both had to come up for air.

Not that he could or would on board ship. Neither was he such a fool that he didn't realize she was up to something. She was. The question was what? And why? Because despite her butter-wouldn't-melt-in-her-mouth smile he had no illusions that he had a long way to go to win Amelia's forgiveness.

"Hey, Dr Stockton," the corpsman greeted her when Amelia stepped into the bay. The young man's eyes ate her up.

Quelling his dislike of another man checking her out, Cole admitted he didn't blame the guy. With her swept-back dark hair exposing the graceful lines of her neck, the luminous quality to her big brown eyes, the fullness of her naturally pink lips, Cole's eyes did some gobbling of their own when Amelia leaned in to examine Corporal Wright's thigh.

"Hmm," she mused, reaching for a pair of disposable gloves. "When I checked you last, the abscess looked better. When did the area start getting worse again?"

"Just last night, Doc. That's why I came back this morning rather than waiting until my follow-up appointment tomorrow." He flashed a flirty smile. "I remembered what you said about coming back sooner if there were any negative changes."

"Good job." Amelia smiled at the man, a real smile, inadvertently jump-starting Cole's heart as surely as if she'd hooked him up to a defibrillator and cranked the juice.

*She used to smile at me like that. Only better.*

Knowing he needed to do something before he succumbed to the errant electrical charges running rampant through his nervous system, Cole gloved up to swab the abscess again.

"Did you see the culture I'd previously done?" she asked, smiling sweetly. Sweetly? Cole didn't know whether to laugh or be afraid. Amelia was a lot of things, but *sweet* wasn't an adjective he'd use to describe her. Unless they were talking about her lips. She had tasted sweet.

"Yes," he answered, studying her, "but your notes say the area was healing well. That's obviously no longer true. I want a new culture."

She flashed her perfectly straight teeth. "Good idea."

Cole managed not to blink. Barely. Had she agreed with him without an argument? Something was definitely up. And not just his temperature and heart rate. He dabbed the swab in the center of the abscess, carefully inserted the tip into the auger filled tube and sealed the lid.

"You think something new is wrong?" the man lying back on the elevated exam table asked, watching as Amelia ungloved and opened a sterile drape, dropped gauze onto the field, poured a small cup of antiseptic solution and opened a package of sterilized scissors, needle holders and toothed tweezers.

"Possibly. That's what the culture will tell us." She opened a bottle of packing gauze and glanced toward Cole. “Do you want to irrigate the area or do you want me to do it?”

Cole hesitated only a millisecond. Despite her sugary sweetness of the past five minutes, Amelia was a take-charge, don’t-put-me-in-the-backseat kind of woman. Even during her residency, she hadn’t liked watching from the sidelines. If he wanted to win her trust he’d have to prove he could deal with her strength and independence, right along with her feigned sugary sweetness.

“You do it,” he told her. “I’ll assist.”

The smile she gave him was so brilliant the sun could have come out in bay two. Definitely his body heated as if the sun had. He was on fire from the inside out.

She donned more gloves, cleaned and irrigated the wound, then packed a thin ribbon of sterile gauze into the opening, leaving the tip out for easier removal.

Watching her work, Cole handed her what she needed before she had to ask. When she was finished and had covered the area with a dressing, she glanced up at him, her eyes sparkling with something that bit deep into him.

"You make an excellent assistant, Cole."

Cole. She called him by his first name rather than Dr Stanley. Hearing his name on her lips made his knees wobble.

Whatever Amelia was up to, he was in trouble. Big trouble.

Because hearing his name on her lips brought back memories of the night he'd gone to her a few weeks after his breakup with Clara. Amelia had whispered his name right before he'd kissed her. As he'd kissed her.

As he'd pushed her back onto her dorm room bed, planning to make love to her.

Rubbing her fingers across Corporal Wright's bandage, Amelia wondered if she was laying her friendliness on too thick? She hadn't meant to be overly nice, but she'd be lying if she didn't admit to enjoying the perplexity in Cole's eyes.

Good. Let him wonder.

Not that he wouldn't figure it out. He'd once known her too well not to know what lengths she'd go to for her crew, for her patients. Still, she welcomed the respite. Carrying around her anger for him was starting to give her an ulcer. At least now she felt as if she was on the offensive.

She much preferred offensive strategies. Always had.

In the grand scheme of personal protection, being nice to Cole for the sake of the crew and their patients wasn't the greatest idea. But a girl had to do what a girl had to do for the greater good.

Besides, it wasn't as if she was going to fall right back into her crush for him. She'd seen what he was capable of. Had seen him bail out on Clara, had seen him walk away from her after a kiss that had singed her toes to the soles of her maid-of-honor high heels. Then walk away from her room after she'd kicked him out, despite her body screaming for him to stay.

Although he'd always seemed to long to be a part of her family, Cole had major commitment issues.

"It'll be a few days before I get the results of the culture back, but I'd like to see you again tomorrow," she told their patient. "Keep your appointment that's already scheduled, and I'll change the dressing."

"Yes, ma'am."

"I think we should change his antibiotic," Cole cut in. He told her the name of an antibiotic with better anaerobic coverage than the antibiotic Corporal Wright currently took.

"Okay, that sounds like a feasible plan." She shot the corpsman another smile. "Take the antibiotics exactly as prescribed and be sure to finish the entire prescription to prevent developing resistance."

"Yes, ma'am."

Cole gave his hand to the corpsman, helped him from the table. Amelia watched the man grimace at the pain that shot up his leg at weight-bearing. She hated it that he'd have to rest in the uncomfortable bunks where he'd have no privacy. As an officer, Amelia had the privilege of sharing a small room with only Suzie, but most of the crew shared large open berths where crew were stacked in so tightly they could barely roll over without bumping the cot above them.

"If you get worse today, make sure you let us know."

"Will do."

The corpsman left the bay and Amelia stared at Cole. He watched her with an inquisitive light in his eyes. One that saw a bit too clearly below the surface.

"What do you think is going on?" she asked, making great effort to keep her voice cordial, pleasant even.

"With Corporal Wright's leg or you?"

Good question. "With Corporal Wright's leg, of course."

"Most likely he has a secondary infection that's spreading into the tissue. If he doesn't respond to the new antibiotic, I'll consider excising the area."

"I doubt that'll be necessary."

"I hope not, but surgical excision would be preferable to him ending up with septicemia or gangrene."

"True." She sucked in a deep breath. "Do you want to stop by and see him with me tomorrow? That way you can decide if surgery should be arranged? You could schedule him if you feel that's the best treatment option."

Eyes narrowing, Cole nodded. "That would be great."

"I'll have Tracy see what time he's supposed to come in."

Amelia turned to step out of the bay, but Cole grabbed her arm. A thousand lightning bolts struck her at once, charring every brain cell to wispy bits of ash.

"About the other?"

"What other?" she gulped, although she knew exactly to what he referred.

"What's going on, Amelia? Did you suddenly decide I deserve forgiveness?"

Forgiveness? She wasn't touching that one.

"You wanted us to work in peace, right?" she challenged, biting her tongue to keep from correcting him on the use of her name. "I can manage being civil for five and a half months."

"Why the change of heart?" He studied her closely.

So closely Amelia wanted to squirm. She didn't.

She held her chin up high and met his gaze head-on in a blatant dare. "Why do you think?"

"Amelia—"

"Hey, Dr Stockton, about that strep patient in bay one?" Tracy poked her head around the curtain, paused when she spotted Cole's hand wrapped around Amelia's upper arm and their low conversation. "Oh, sorry, I didn't mean to interrupt."

"No interruption," Amelia assured her, smiling appreciatively at her nurse. "I'm on my way to check the strep patient. Tell Richard to bring back the next patient, and, Tracy, could you let Dr Stanley know what time Corporal Wright will be by tomorrow for his follow-up? If he's not in surgery, he'll have a quick look at the patient."

# CHAPTER FIVE

NEAR the end of Amelia's shift, a corpsman was brought in who'd slammed his fingers in a hatch during a training exercise.

Amazingly his X-ray didn't show any displaced breaks, only a hairline fracture of the proximal phalange of the index finger, which wouldn't require an off ship consult with an orthopedic.

After washing her hands and donning gloves, Amelia removed the bloody towel pressed over the man's hand. She didn't wince at the bleeding, macerated tissue. She'd been trained to see far worse than the man's sliced-open, deformed fingers.

"I hope the other guy looks worse," she teased, hoping to ease the strain from his face. An aircraft carrier with its ladders, hatches and catapults was a host of injuries waiting to happen. Unfortunately.

"Not even a scratch," the man responded, his eyes not leaving his injuries.

Where the heavy metal hatch had come across the top of his fingers, the skin was split in a deep gash. Amelia dabbed away blood with sterile gauze, seeing bone through the mangled flesh of his index and middle fingers. The cuts on his ring finger and pinky didn't appear to have reached the bone.

She turned to Tracy. "Set up two suture trays. I'm going to ask Dr Stanley to help with the two deeper wounds as they're more extensive."

Although her eyes widened, Tracy just nodded and went about setting up the trays.

Amelia explained what she was going to do to her patient then left the bay to find Cole. Technically, he should have left the medical ward hours ago. Instead, as he'd done each day since arriving, he'd hung around.

Now he stood across the sick ward, talking to Richard, Peyton, who was the ship's nurse anesthetist, and the physician assistant. As if sensing Amelia, he glanced up, met her gaze, and grinned. Why did her heart light up at his smile?

She was just tolerating him to keep things running smoothly in her medical ward. She didn't like him, didn't enjoy being in his company, didn't even want him there.

But she'd been crazy about him once upon a time.

Crazy about him in the worst kind of way because she had liked him, had enjoyed being in his company, had wanted to spend as much time as possible with him because he'd made her smile, laugh, look at life in Technicolor.

She'd denied just how much the way he affected her had meant, had denied she'd cared more for him than she should have. On the night of the wedding rehearsal, she'd quit denying. And look how that had ended up—two Stockton hearts broken in one night. What a fool she'd been.

Even now, looking at him, unable to suppress the quivers low in her belly, she wondered if she was just as much a fool.

"I need your help," she said, shoving aside her self-preservation instincts.

Immediately, he stepped away from the men

he'd been talking to. "I'm yours. All you have to do is ask."

She so wasn't touching his comment, but her imagination toyed with the double entendre. Had he intentionally sent her thoughts into a whirlwind?

"I have a hand injury that's going to require multiple sutures. Capillary refill is good in all fingers. Sensation is decreased. There's a hairline fracture in the index finger, but no other breaks. I was hoping you'd have a look. The index and middle fingers will require more extensive suturing."

"Sure." Cole followed her into the bay. While he washed his hands, he introduced himself to the injured corpsman. He examined the patient then turned to Amelia. "You're right about the first two fingers. I'll suture them."

She could do them, Amelia wanted to argue. But this wasn't about what she could and could not do. This was about proving to her crew that she wouldn't compromise them or their patients, that she could set aside her personal feelings because she was a professional, a Stockton.

"I was hoping you'd offer." And not because he really could do a better job on the man's fingers. She might be trying to make a point, but she didn't plan to beg Cole just to prove to her crew that she was a team player.

"Like I said..." his gaze sought hers "...I'm all yours."

Still not acknowledging his comment, she smiled at the pale man. "Dr Stanley is the ship's surgeon. He'll do an excellent job on those fingers while I sew the other two up so we get you put back together a little quicker."

With Tracy and Richard assisting and the man's fingers spread wide, Amelia and Cole worked from opposite sides of the exam table, slowly closing the man's wounds. Their workspace was tight due to the close proximity of the injuries, but just as they'd done earlier, done years ago, they worked well together, rarely encroaching on each other's space.

From time to time, Amelia would sense Cole glancing up, toward her, but for the most part their concentration centered directly on their patient and his well-being.

Amelia had asked Tracy to give the man something for pain prior to starting the closure. Between the narcotic and the local anesthetic at the injury site, the man seemed comfortable. Actually, Amelia was fairly positive near the end of the procedure that he'd fallen asleep.

She finished the less extensive lacerations on his pinky and ring fingers prior to Cole finishing the deeper wounds.

She turned to the nurse and Richard. "I'll assist Dr Stanley. If there are no more patients, you both can go ahead and sign out for the day. Thanks for all your assistance."

Sharing a stunned glance, Tracy and the corpsman left the bay to finish their day's duties.

"I'm glad you asked me to help," Cole told her when they were alone. "It was just like old times."

Old times when she'd been an eager resident and he'd allowed her to sit in on procedures to give her the experience.

"You'd have been here another hour at least if you hadn't."

"Saving time wasn't why I asked you to help."

"So why did you?" Pulling the ethilon thread through, Cole's gaze lifted to hers, his blue eyes twinkling with a teasing quality that made her almost giddy. "Because you knew I was a better seamstress?"

"No." Prior to seeing his handiwork on the man's lacerations she might have argued that these days she could out-suture him. She was good, but Cole was doing a great job of repairing the man's wounds. As much as she hated to admit it, she couldn't have done better. "That isn't why I asked, either."

Wondering why her insides shook when what he thought of her didn't matter. Neither should that twinkle in his eyes make her want to smile in return. She shouldn't want to smile at him, shouldn't feel lighter because he was teasing her.

But she did.

"Tracy told me I was treating you unfairly and should let go of the past."

"I see." Keeping his gaze trained on his handiwork, he looped the needle back through the sleeping corpsman's flesh. "How did you respond?"

He'd already seen her response. He knew she was going to set aside her aversion of him for the better of the crew. But he'd asked because he wanted her to tell him one on one that she was ready to let the past go, for them to develop an amicable working relationship. Amelia wanted to dislike him all the more for it, but found she couldn't. Not when he seemed so genuinely pleased, as if she'd done him some great favor.

"She's right."

His hands stilled for a brief moment, shook ever so slightly.

Amelia hated the tremor that shook her own body in response. Why was she so in tune with Cole? Why did being here with him feel so right? And so very wrong?

"You were right," she admitted.

"About?"

*Everything you said to me on the night you came to my dorm.*

No, he hadn't been right about that.

There could be nothing between them. Not physically. Not emotionally. Not anything. Nothing except the need to work amicably together for the next few months.

So why had she just thought about that night again?

She took a deep breath. "The first day you were on board you told me we'd have to come to some type of peace or our past would affect our jobs."

He looped the needle through the patient's gaping flesh, pulled it the rest of the way through with the needle holders.

"Obviously, I wasn't as good at hiding my feelings toward you as I'd hoped. The crew thinks I don't like you for some reason." She said the last with a slight lilt to her voice, as if she couldn't fathom what had given them that idea. "I do think you're a great surgeon, for whatever that's worth." She nodded toward where he was closing the last wound. "And a fabulous seamstress. I'm impressed with how neatly you were able to pull his lacerations on his index finger back together. I couldn't have done a better job."

He didn't look at her, just kept his gaze on

his work. "My ability to outsew you makes me forgiven?"

"No," she denied, knowing he wouldn't buy it even if she lied. "I never said you were forgiven. I'm not sure I can forgive you. But for the duration of us working together, I'm willing to negotiate a peace treaty, so to speak."

He seemed to consider her offer. "For the benefit of our coworkers?"

"Hey." She tried to make light of it. "From time to time even sworn enemies have agreed to coexist for the greater good."

He pulled the thread back through and examined the now closed wound. Satisfied with his work, he wrapped the thread around the end of the needle holder several times, pulled the thread tight and tied off a knot. He then repeated the process several times, changing direction of the rotation of thread each time to strengthen the knot.

When he'd finished, Amelia handed him a pair of suture scissors. He cut the line, leaving only a few millimeters of thread above the knot, just enough to make removal easier.

"You're an interesting woman, Amelia Stockton. Generous to a fault." Generous to a fault? What was he saying? "But, for the record, you've never been my enemy. Neither have I been yours."

Amelia's breath caught.

Rather than look at her, Cole gently shook the dozing man's arm. "Paul? Wake up. We're finished closing the lacerations."

Slowly the man's eyes blinked open, adjusting bit by bit to his environment.

"It's okay that you aren't feeling much, if anything, in your fingers. Your hand is still numb from the anesthetic. I need you to make a fist then flatten your hand for me so I can check your range of motion."

The man did as asked.

"Excellent," Cole praised, taking hold of the needle holder and blocking Paul's vision of his hand. "I'm going to touch each of your fingers and without looking I need you to tell me when I'm touching you, if you can. Just like we did before we started to sew. Again, you still have anesthesia on board, so don't be alarmed if you don't feel anything yet." Cole grinned. "Actually, be grateful if the numbness lasts a while."

Sensation in the tip of Paul's pinky was normal, but there was still nothing in the other three lacerated fingers.

"It's not uncommon after an injury like this to have decreased sensation," Cole explained. "I didn't see any evidence of a lacerated nerve, but with the weight of the hatch crushing your fingers, it's possible."

Wincing, the man moved his fingers back and forth, studying the suture lines. "What if it isn't the anesthesia causing the numbness? Will I get the feeling back?"

"In most cases sensation will return on its own within a few days to weeks. However, we will need to keep a close watch on you," Cole told the pale, slightly dazed man. "I'm going to give you an antibiotic prophylaxis and something for pain, but you'll need to return to the sick ward tomorrow morning for a checkup."

Cole helped walk the man out of the bay.

Through the screen, Amelia heard him speak to a corpsman regarding getting the man safely to his berth. Cole was a thoughtful surgeon, caring of his patients. He always had been.

Trying to keep her thoughts off his comment about not being her enemy, she emptied the surgical trays, properly disposing of the sharps and contaminated materials used, saving everything that could be sterilized for future use. She was wiping down the metal tray when Cole stepped back behind the curtain.

"There aren't any more patients to be seen today," he informed her, leaning against the counter. His hair was tousled, his eyes intensely blue, his smile contagious.

God, he really was Dr Delicious.

No, no, Dr Disastrous. She had to remember that.

"Okay." Uncertain about her truce, she studied where her hands wiped the tray. Was she crazy to think she could be amicable to Cole after the way he'd hurt her sister? Or were her fears anything to do with her sister? Were her fears more wrapped up in the fact that her heart pounded against her rib cage like an out-of-control monster wanting out of its cage?

She glanced up, met his gaze, held her breath. Why did he affect her so crazily?

"Are you going to the gym?" He pushed off the counter, straightening to his full height of over six feet, making her feel small and feminine. "I'll see you there."

He hadn't had to wait for her answer. He knew she was. She always worked out after finishing in clinic. So did he, at exactly the same time. Actually, Cole seemed to be on the same wavelength with her on a lot of things. If she went for a walk on the "steel beach," so did he. If she went to the exercise room, so did he. When she arrived at the dining hall, so did he. The only time she'd had peace was while inside her room and calling being alone with her thoughts peaceful was stretching the truth to say the least.

There wasn't anything peaceful about closing her eyes and dreaming of the man gazing so intently at her.

Amelia was having a difficult time breathing, but not because of her workout routine. More like because of the man on the elliptical in front of her.

The very hot man wearing workout shorts and a form-fitting navy blue T-shirt that made his arms look ripped and hinted at abs worthy of a men's fitness magazine.

Not that she was looking at his abs.

No, she was facing his backside. His tight glutes, his sinewy thighs, his rock-hard calves, his—

"You're staring again," Suzie warned in a low voice so as not to be overheard in the semicrowded workout room.

Amelia shot a dirty look at her friend. "I'm looking straight ahead. Not staring."

"Sure, you're not staring. Neither am I." Her roommate snickered, waggling her eyebrows in Cole's direction.

The machine next to Amelia had been occupied by a captain when Cole had arrived. He'd taken a machine in front of Amelia and slightly to her right. Seriously, just looking straight ahead, she couldn't possibly not look at him unless she closed her eyes. And, really, who ever heard of exercising with your eyes closed?

"You have to admit," Suzie continued, obviously enjoying herself. "The view is mouthwatering."

Wiping her forearm across her sweaty face, Amelia rolled her eyes. "You have such a one-track mind."

Waggling her eyebrows again, Suzie laughed. "Absolutely. Tell me that isn't one fine specimen of man in front of us."

Amelia couldn't. Cole was one fine specimen of man.

If she'd met him for the first time on board the USS *Benjamin Franklin*, she'd have liked Cole. A lot. He was witty, helpful, generous, intelligent, charming, *sexy*.

If she'd just met Cole she'd be half in love with him.

Only she hadn't just met him. She'd met him years ago as her sister's fiancé. Clara had been deceived by Cole's false wonderfulness, too. What would her sister say if she knew Amelia was being suckered in by her ex-fiancé? That she'd been suckered in years ago and wondered if she'd truly ever gotten over her infatuation with him?

"You know, if I didn't know better, I'd think you were softening where he's concerned."

Amelia shot another glare at her bunkmate. "You'd be wrong if you thought that."

Okay, so she'd just been thinking she was being suckered in, but no way would she admit that out loud.

"Would I?" Suzie asked, her thin black brow arched high.

"Just because I have to work with him, it doesn't mean I like him." Or that she couldn't appreciate his positives.

Suzie and Amelia both turned back to stare ahead. At Cole.

His calves were taut as his legs worked up and down. Sweat dampened his T-shirt, causing the cotton material to cling to his back, his well-defined back that tapered from wide shoulders to a narrow waist to tight buttocks and strong thighs. Oh, *heaven*.

Amelia's tongue stuck to the roof of her mouth.

Okay, Cole was hotter than the Sahara Desert.

Way hotter.

She even found the sweat glistening on his skin

and dampening his T-shirt oddly appealing. What was wrong with her? She did not find sweaty, overheated men appealing.

Amelia's machine beeped, indicating she'd hit peak speed.

"I heard you and he talked today," Suzie pressed, glancing toward the control panel on Amelia's elliptical and whistling.

"You heard that?" She tried to drag her gaze away from Cole. And failed. Which was okay, since she was only looking straight ahead, right? To not look at him she'd have to twist her head and that would be poor body mechanics.

Never let it be said a Stockton had poor body mechanics.

"Oh, yeah." Suzie laughed. "I heard that and more."

"More?" Amelia gulped, knowing she was the butt of ship gossip. *Great.* "What more?"

"You think everyone in Medical hasn't seen the way he looks at you? That they haven't noticed the way you watch him when you think they aren't paying attention?" Tsking, Suzie shook her head. "You should know better than to think you could get away with something like that."

"How does he look at me?"

Suzie's lips curled upwards. "Of everything I said, that's what caught your attention? That he looks at you?"

She shouldn't care, shouldn't be holding her breath, waiting. Should be more concerned that others had noticed. Yet…

"How does he look at me?" she stage-whispered, her gaze finally managing to shift from Cole to her bunkmate.

Suzie's black eyes bored into Amelia, her voice purred with envy. "Like he wants to dip you in chocolate and nibble his way to the center."

Amelia let that digest, fought to control the tiny spurts of anxiety. They were spurts of anxiety, not hope.

"Amelia?" Suzie questioned when she didn't respond.

"He doesn't want to do that to me," she denied, because she couldn't verbalize that Cole wanted her, that deep down she wanted him to want her. How could she want Cole to dip her in chocolate and nibble his way to her center? That would be wrong on so many counts. "That's crazy. Cole can't want me."

Because if he did, how would she deal with her own treacherous unresolved feelings?

"I wouldn't say that."

Both women jumped at Cole's voice.

When had he stepped off the machine? Walked over to them?

What did he mean, he wouldn't say that?

"You were listening to our private conversation?" Amelia snapped, her face flushing. Was he admitting to wanting her? If so, what did that mean? What did she want it to mean?

"If you didn't want me to listen, you shouldn't have been talking where I could hear." His gaze didn't leave hers. "Why can't I want you, Amelia? I told you I wanted you. Two years ago. Have you forgotten?"

This couldn't be happening. Shouldn't be happening. Why was Suzie smiling like the fool cat that ate the canary?

"You heard everything we said?"

"Not everything." His gaze went back and forth

between the two women, his gaze settling back on Amelia. "But enough."

"Enough." He'd heard her question Suzie about how he looked at her. Her face burned in shame. *Oh, Clara, I'm sorry. I'll get whatever this hold he has over me under control.*

Amelia stopped moving on the machine, gave Suzie a dirty look, then walked toward the weights.

Cole followed her.

"I owe you an apology," she said stiffly when he stood next to her. "Suzie and I shouldn't have been discussing you."

"Maybe you haven't noticed, but I'm not complaining." The corner of his mouth lifted in a crooked smile and his eyes sparked with mischief. "You can discuss me anytime."

Amelia placed her hand on the weight rack, reluctantly met Cole's gaze.

She had to remember her sister, had to ignore the excited bubbles working their way through her like a pot of boiling water.

"What are we doing, Cole?"

His grin was contagious, but she pretended immunity.

"Working out?" he offered.

She sighed at his deliberate misunderstanding of what she'd asked. "I may have agreed to a truce for the sake of the crew, but that's as far as this goes."

His expression sobering, he nodded. "That truce is more than I expected, Amelia, but I'd be lying if I didn't admit to wanting more."

There went her heart rate again.

"What kind of more?" she dared ask, for the simple reason she couldn't not ask.

She knew what he was going to say, knew she wasn't prepared for his answer, knew she needed to put some distance between them right this very second.

Instead she stood still, her fingers curled around a dumbbell, waiting for him to say words she didn't want to hear, and yet she did want to hear them. Over and over.

And that made her weak, something she couldn't stand being, a failure in her own eyes. A failure to her self and to her family.

What would her family say if they knew she and Cole had kissed between the wedding rehearsal and the time he'd broken things off with Clara? What would Clara say?

Amelia couldn't bear to hurt her family, but she couldn't turn away from Cole. She stood her ground, waiting for words she hadn't heard in two years and yet had never been able to forget, had awakened in cold sweats hearing them echo through her dreams. Words she needed to hear again, even if for just one last time.

*Clara, forgive me for what I'm feeling.*

She held her breath, her lungs threatening to burst, her ears straining to hear his answer, wanting to believe he meant what he said and that he wasn't there because of some twisted reason to do with her sister.

"I want you."

# CHAPTER SIX

AMELIA'S breath gushed out at the bombshell Cole dropped between them. "What do you mean, you want me?"

He stared down into Amelia's big brown eyes and thought her the most beautiful woman he'd ever seen. Yes, her hair was swept up in its usual ponytail and sweat glistened across her brow and ran down her neck, but she was beautiful.

Maybe because of the way those big brown eyes stared up at him. Maybe because of the way there was a growing acknowledgment that neither of them could stop what was happening between them, just as they hadn't been able to stop what had grown unbidden between them years ago.

A friendship that had developed into something much deeper.

"You know what I mean."

"Do I?" Her chin lifted, letting him know she wouldn't go down without a fight.

When would she figure out fighting with her was the last thing he wanted?

"I told you how I felt about you."

"The night you came to my dorm room and declared you'd fallen into lust with me despite the fact you'd been scheduled to walk down the aisle with my sister?"

He winced. Was that how she'd taken his confession that night? Lust? He wanted to deny the crude description, but she was right. He had felt an undeniable physical attraction to her, but lust didn't begin to cover the depth of his feelings.

"That isn't what I said."

"No?" Her brow arched and her chin raised another defensive notch. "That's distinctly how I remember your pitiful attempt to get into my bed that night."

"Pitiful?" A blast of wounded pride hit him. "It worked, didn't it?"

Her eyes narrowed with renewed anger and Cole instantly wished he could take back his biting words.

"You may have gotten into my bed." She spoke low, succinctly, coldly. "But I came to my senses before any real damage occurred."

Yes, she'd stopped him, told him she never wanted to see him again. Ever. She'd told him she hated him. She had hated him. Of that, Cole couldn't be mistaken. The look in her eyes when she'd ordered him out of her life had been murderous.

That look was what had kept him away from her for the past two years. What man wanted to put himself in the line of fire for sure rejection?

Yet wasn't that what he'd done by coming aboard her ship? By putting his career on the line to do so?

He couldn't explain that one even to himself.

He glanced around at the other crew working out. No one seemed to be paying them the slightest attention, except for Suzie, and even she was out of earshot as long as they kept their voices low. Still, their conversation wasn't meant for possible public consumption.

"This isn't the time or place for this discussion."

Seeming to recall where they were, Amelia took a measured breath, her chest rising and falling with remembered anger. They'd made progress today, in the sick ward, but now she looked ready to rip her peace treaty to shreds and declare all-out war.

"I'm not sure we should ever have this particular conversation," she said between straight, gritted teeth.

"Make no mistake. This is one conversation that's long overdue and unavoidable." One they should have had years ago. "Eventually, we'll have to face what's between us. Past and present." But she wasn't ready to admit as much yet and he'd been a fool to try to push her into doing so. "It would be nice if we could forget everything we knew about each other and start over. Without the past clouding the way you view me."

"Short of a case of amnesia, I don't see that as a possibility, do you?"

"You want me to hit you over the head and see if that works?" he offered, half-serious as if he thought that would erase the past, clear the slate. He wanted the opportunity to get to know Amelia, to explore the attraction between them.

"Just being near you is like constantly being hit over the head," she muttered, not looking at him.

"With good thoughts?"

"With thoughts of how much I'd like to hit you over the head."

He laughed.

"That wasn't supposed to be funny," she warned, but when her gaze met his, a smile twisted her lips.

Cole's body lit like a Fourth of July celebration. And just as quickly fizzled out when Amelia's expression tightened and she desperately began setting up boundaries again, terms to their peace treaty.

"Look, you were right about us having to set aside the past while working together. I've already admitted that. But that doesn't mean I want to be your friend or to recapture whatever was between us." She stared him straight in the eyes. "I don't. What happened in the past just needs to stay in the past."

Disappointment and frustration hit him. When he opened his mouth to say more, she shook her head at him.

"Whatever it is you want from me, Cole, it isn't going to happen."

"How do you know?" he pushed, obviously shocking her Stockton good sense. "How can you be so sure that what I want isn't going to happen?"

He wasn't sure about anything where she was concerned. Then again, he'd never had to work to gain a woman's good favor before. Women had always come to him, never mattered one way or the other.

Except Amelia.

"I just know," she stubbornly replied, dropping her free weight back onto the rack and glaring at him.

"Because you aren't willing to give me a chance?"

Looking totally exasperated, she faced him with her hands on her hips and her eyes full of fire. "A chance at what? What is it you want?"

"You."

She shook her head. "What kind of game are you playing?"

Is that what she thought? That he was playing with her? He wanted her, was honest enough to admit to that want, and she thought he was playing games? But what about her? Because for all her bluster, for all the hatred that blazed in her eyes, desire blazed just as strongly. She could deny it all she wanted, but Amelia wanted him every bit as much as he wanted her.

Glancing around the workout room, he noticed they'd started to attract some attention.

"Let's go somewhere we can talk in private, Amelia."

Looking as if she planned to run and never look back, she shook her head. "I agreed to a truce for professional reasons, Cole. Nothing more. If you have some sister fantasy or are just trying to use me to get to Clara, get over it. You are the last man I'd ever willingly become involved with. Understand?"

With that, she spun, swishing her ponytail at him, and walked away, leaving him to wonder why he couldn't have left well enough alone, biding his time and accepting the progress they'd made today instead of pushing for more.

But he knew.

The more time he spent with Amelia, the more he wanted her, the harder not pushing became.

He'd only been on board a few weeks. He had over five months to go. Five months of being with Amelia, of convincing her to give him a chance so he could work out the crazy hold she held over him.

Five months.

It seemed like no time at all.

It seemed like forever.

Why did Amelia think him being here had anything to do with Clara? All he wanted was for her to forget he and Clara had ever been engaged so Amelia could see the potential of him and her.

Sister fantasy indeed.

There wasn't room in his fantasies for anyone other than Amelia and hadn't been for years.

Six weeks into his deployment, Cole shined the light into a soldier's eyes, watching the reflexive size change in response. Perfect. He looked in ears, making note of bulging red tympanic membranes, checked nostrils that revealed swollen mucosa and purulent drainage. He checked a throat that was beefy red, raw.

Running his fingertips over the man's cervical lymph nodes, he felt swollen glands. "That sore?"

Wincing, the man nodded.

The soldier's submandibular, pre- and post-cervical and auricular nodes were all enlarged and tender.

The man's heart rate was increased, but that wasn't uncommon when febrile. Lungs sounded raspy with a soft inspiratory wheeze in both lower lobes. There was no abdominal tenderness, although the man had reported some digestive trouble over the past twenty-four hours.

"I'm going to start you on medication." Cole told him the names of the medicines and what each was for.

The man nodded his understanding.

"Unfortunately, you are infectious. I can't let you return to your berthing quarters."

Nodding, the man looked as if he'd expected as much. "I'll be sleeping in quarantine?"

"Yes." Cole let his nurse know the man would need to be put in quarantine, along with several others who were also suffering from the virus that had hit the ship. Keeping the virus from spreading to the rest of the crew was of paramount importance.

"There's an abdominal pain in bay one. Lieutenant Sanchez," Richard informed him. "Dr Stockton is in with her. She asked for a consult when you finished."

Amelia. With the viral outbreak, they'd been so busy they'd not had any more serious talks, only skimmed the surface, being cordial, being polite, only occasional unguarded glances hinting at what lay beneath.

"Knock, knock," Cole said, rounding the curtain to enter bay one and take in the scene before him.

Amelia looked fabulous in her khaki pants and navy knit shirt, the collar turned down at the base of her throat. Her hair was up in a ponytail and her eyes held compassion as she examined her patient.

A softly crying pretty Hispanic woman lay on the exam table, her arms crossed protectively over her ample chest.

Having been bent over the woman, stethoscope in her ears while listening to the woman's lower abdomen, Amelia glanced up, seeming surprised to see him. She straightened. "I'm sorry, Dr Stanley, but I don't need your help after all."

"You're sure?" Cole's brows drew together. She didn't want him to consult? Were they reverting back to that? He didn't buy it. Amelia was a wonderful doctor, one Cole trusted implicitly. Her professionalism and ethics wouldn't allow her to put a patient at risk for personal reasons. "It's no problem for me to have a quick look."

She shook her head, conveying with her eyes that she'd like him to leave without making a big deal of it. What was going on?

Making a quick decision, he shrugged. "If you need me, you know where to find me."

"Thanks." She waved him out and turned her attention back to her patient.

Half an hour later, he caught her coming out of the medical office. “Earlier, you released the abdominal pain without observation. False alarm?”

“Not really.” She didn’t meet his eyes, which sent up warning flags left and right.

“What was wrong?”

“I’d rather not discuss my patient.”

He eyed her curiously.

“Look,” she began, “it’s not my place to tell you. There are a few things on this ship that are still private, believe it or not. I won’t break patient confidentiality unnecessarily.”

“How is consulting with me about an abdominal pain patient a breach of confidentiality?” he asked in frustration. “I’m the surgeon.”

“Not all abdominal pains require a surgeon.”

“This one didn’t?”

“Obviously not or I would have gotten you to check her rather than asking you to leave.”

“Obviously.”

She hesitated a moment, her expression softening, reeling him in without even realizing that’s what she was doing.

"Thanks for not making a scene in front of the patient. I was afraid you'd insist on checking her." She met his gaze. "I appreciate that you did the right thing, letting me do my job."

At her tentative smile, the ship shifted beneath his feet. "When is she coming back for follow-up?"

Again, a slight hesitation. "She'll come back if needed, but she's putting in for a reassignment."

A reassignment? "Sea life not for her?"

"Not everyone takes to ship life."

Which they would have discovered during the many training exercises prior to deployment. Interesting.

"She was suffering from seasickness?" he asked, wondering if Amelia would lie to him. Although he didn't know what had been bothering the woman, he did know seasickness wasn't a likely diagnosis.

"No, she's been aboard the ship for some time, but…" She paused, glanced at him and then shrugged. "Let's talk about something else. How are you holding up? Lots of viral patients?"

Cole studied her, admired her for protecting her

patient, even though she should know she didn't have to protect the woman from him. Probably an STD, likely pelvic inflammatory disease or something similar, possibly even pregnancy, since Amelia was being so secretive.

"More than I'd like. If we can't get this quarantined, we're going to have an epidemic on our hands."

She ran her fingers through her ponytail then tightened the elastic band. "That's what I'm afraid of. I saw mostly viral patients during sick call this morning, too. The senior medical officer has put out an advisory for everyone to come in at the first sign of symptoms so we can stop the spread."

Watching the play of light hit her shiny dark hair, wishing he could run his fingers through the silky gloss, could lean down and breathe in the scent of her shampoo, the scent of her, Cole gave a wry smile. "Which means the medical crew is going to be all the busier."

Returning his smile, she nodded. "Yes, sir. You sure you want to stick around for this?"

His gaze met hers, sent a thousand silent

messages, asked a thousand questions, all of which Amelia didn't respond to. If only she'd tell him what was in her mind. Did her body heat up the way his did any time they were near each other? Did every sense become sharper, more alert, more aware, the way his did?

Of course, she didn't answer any of those questions and he couldn't voice them. Not yet. All he could do was smile at her and hope that with time whatever was between them would come to a head and free them both.

"There's nowhere I'd rather be than right here," he admitted, watching the color of her eyes darken to rich melted chocolate, watching her full pink lips part, and a short gust of air escape. "With you, Amelia. Nowhere else."

# CHAPTER SEVEN

ONE day at a time, Amelia reminded herself later that day. One day at a time. That's how she'd deal with Cole. How she was dealing with him, and how she'd continue to deal with him.

So far she was six weeks down and twenty more to go. That was only one hundred and forty days, give or take a few pending either of their reassignments.

Not that she was counting.

Sighing, she glanced across the sick ward to where he stood, laughing at a joke the physician assistant had told. Tracy, Richard, Peyton and a couple of nurses and corpsmen stood with them. So did the senior medical officer. Despite the crazily busy day they'd had, they all looked relaxed, if a bit tired. They all looked toward Cole with respect and admiration, with friendship.

Cole belonged on board the USS *Benjamin*

*Franklin* as much as if he'd been there from the day the ship had first sailed for training exercises.

As much as she hated to admit it, she'd grown to appreciate his presence in the sick ward, too.

They'd had another swamped sick call, which had run over into the scheduled appointments. A nasty upper respiratory virus was running rampant across the ship. If Cole hadn't been there to help, following his surgery clinic, none of them would be anywhere near finished. They'd all had their hands full, mostly with viral patients but also with the usual plethora of cases as well.

Then there had been the young lieutenant who worked in the ship operations department and suffered from abdominal pain. Although the carrier intelligence center officer's diagnosis hadn't been anything out of the ordinary in the grand scheme of life occurrences, the diagnosis wasn't one Amelia commonly made. Actually, she hadn't diagnosed a pregnancy in months.

The woman hadn't wanted to put down that she thought she was pregnant, had begged Amelia to keep her secret until she'd figured out the course of action she wanted to take and for Amelia to please honor her wishes. The woman had likely had an on board affair with another officer and was fearful of both of them facing dishonorable discharge.

Regardless of her reasons, Amelia had hedged the best she could. Only she and the lab technician who'd performed the test knew the woman's real reason for visiting the sick ward.

She partially owed thanks to Cole for that. Had she realized the woman's true reasons for the visit she wouldn't have requested the consult, but she hadn't known prior to their private discussion.

Cole had deferred to her request. Would his predecessor have done so? She doubted it. Not only had the man who'd gone through the training exercises with the ship been higher ranked but Dr Evans had been full of arrogance as well. He'd have insisted on checking the woman.

Cole didn't pull rank. He listened, really listened. Just as he'd always listened to her. Whether in regard to a particular professor or a recount of her rounds, Cole had always had time to listen, to offer advice or guidance. He'd smile, offer a comforting word, a gentle pat of his hand across hers.

And she'd wanted more. Even in the earliest of days, she'd wanted Cole. Had been aware of everything about him. She'd denied her feelings, of course, even to herself. How could she not have when he'd belonged to Clara?

Even now, when she didn't want to like anything in regards to Cole, she was finding way too many things to like.

The way he smiled, the way he volunteered to help, the way he interacted with the crew, the way he threw himself one hundred percent into everything he did, the way he looked at her as if she were the only thing he saw.

Yesterday in the gym, while she and Suzie had put their time in on the elliptical, with him on the machine next to theirs, she'd found herself laughing at his corny jokes.

And when had he fallen into sitting with them in the dinner wardroom each night? When had she stopped resenting him for doing so? When had she started looking forward to the moment he joined their table, adding a flavor to the meals no cook could produce?

Remembering that she didn't like him was getting more and more difficult because, darn it, he was likeable.

More than likeable.

How could she like him when she was swamped with guilt? When each and every smile that passed between Cole and herself was a betrayal to her sister?

She ran her fingers through her hair, catching his gaze as he glanced up from the group he was talking to. He wore navy pants and shirt with the navy medical logo on the left breast. The color only intensified the blueness of his eyes, making her think of childhood days of playing beneath a cloudless sky. That's what Cole was. A sunny day. Only his sunshine was deceptive, more dangerous, threatening to burn her to ashes.

"Did you hear what Peyton said?" he asked, his smile lethal.

How was it possible for him to look so great when he should be dead on his feet? She must look like death warmed over. Yet he looked as if he could pull another clinic without batting an eyelash.

Amazed by his endless energy, she shook her head. “I think my ears are too tired to hear anything other than the call of my pillow.”

Concern flickered in his eyes. “You okay? You’re not coming down with the virus are you?”

She shook her head. “I’m just tired.”

*And disgusted with myself that I’m falling for your charms all over again even though I know better.*

Analyzing every feature to the point she felt as if she should put her hands in front her face, he didn’t look convinced. “You shouldn’t have worked through lunch.”

“I didn’t do anything you didn’t do,” she reminded him.

Despite the fact that he didn’t have to be there, Cole worked just as hard as the rest of them.

“I don’t know about the rest of you, but I’m headed for a shower, then to grab something to eat.” Tracy spoke, tossing her stethoscope down on the counter. “I’ll see you guys in the morning.

Let's pray this virus passes quickly and doesn't take hold of any of us."

Amelia nodded, as did the rest of the crew as they broke up, each heading their own way, until the sick ward became eerily quiet.

Only she and Cole remained.

Slowly, as if he had all the time in the world, Cole crossed the room to stand close. Too close.

Running her hand over her tight neck muscles, she held her ground, pretended like his nearness didn't make her nervous. "Thanks for your help today."

"You're welcome." His response was low, husky, a bit succinct for a man who seemed to search for things to talk to her about.

The only sound in the room was the lub-dub of Amelia's ticking heart. Ticking? Ha. More like ba-booming. That ba-boom was probably rocking the entire ship, causing tidal waves on far-away shores.

She stared at him, wondering at why he'd crossed the room, wondering at his silence, wondering at her foolishness for just standing there, waiting, for what?

Although they hadn't had another talk about the past, she could honestly say there hadn't been many awkward silences. Mostly because Cole always said something to fill any conversation void that arose. Something smart, witty, flirty, complimentary, *something*.

Now he didn't say anything. Not a word.

Standing with only a couple of feet between them, he just looked at her. Really, really looked at her.

Her whole body trembled and she knew something monumental was about to happen. She could see it in his eyes. Could feel it in the way his body called to hers.

After weeks of skimming the surface, of letting her pretend she was off the hook and that he'd go along with their truce and ignore the underlying currents, Cole wasn't planning to play nice.

"I'm sorry, Amelia."

She bit the inside of her lower lip, wishing he hadn't broken the silence, not with those words, words that penetrated deeper than any missile.

"What for? You were great today." Even as she said the words, she knew he wasn't talking about today. She knew exactly what he was talking about and she didn't want to discuss the past, wanted to keep her tone light and easygoing.

But Cole had obviously reached a breaking point.

"For kissing you, for leaving, for coming to your dorm that night, for hurting you and your family, for not being able to stay away from you even though it's what you said you wanted." He took a deep breath. "I'm sorry for every mistake I've made."

No, she didn't want to hear his apology, didn't want to feel the forgiveness welling in her heart.

Stocktons didn't forgive, they got even.

Yet that didn't feel right either.

"Why did you come?" she asked, needing to know what had driven him to show up at her dorm that crazy night so long ago when he'd obviously had no problems leaving her waiting on the night of his rehearsal. "Surely you didn't believe I'd welcome you? Not after what happened?"

"I couldn't not come." Stepping even closer, he grazed his knuckles across her cheek as if he also couldn't not touch her. "I tried to stay away, because I knew you wouldn't forgive me. That was a given." His fingers paused, tensing against her skin. "How could you? But I couldn't stay away."

Amelia fought leaning into his touch, fought the maelstrom of emotions swirling within her. She held his gaze, thinking him more dangerous to her well-being than any mission she might ever undertake. "Because?"

Of Clara? she wanted to ask, but couldn't. When he looked at her as if he wanted her so badly, surely he wasn't thinking of her sister?

"You were all I could think about, that I'd asked you to wait for me." His palm cupped her face, his gaze bore into hers. "You're still all I think about."

Bells blared in her head, warning *danger, danger.* But he hadn't said Clara, he'd said you, as in her. Not her sister. Her. Amelia.

Even as giddiness bubbled inside her, she had to stop him. Whether he was using her or not was irrelevant in the grand scheme of things. Cole had taken the cowardly way out, walking away. She could never respect that.

"Cole, don't do this."

*Please don't do this.*

But he didn't move away, only caressed her cheek as if she was the most precious thing he'd ever touched. "This? Is this what you don't want me to do? I can't deny it anymore, Amelia. I want to touch you. I've always wanted to touch you. You felt the heat between us as surely as I did."

"Don't say these things." *Don't touch me. I can't think when you do.*

"Why not?" His thumb brushed back and forth in a slow stroke across her tingling flesh, leaving a trail of fire that burned clear to her core. "They're true. I've never stopped thinking about you, wanting you. The moment I saw you again, I knew I was right to come here."

The blaring bells cleared enough for a new warning to pop into her head, one that told her she hadn't given Cole nearly enough credit for being the master strategist he so obviously was. She felt sucker punched.

"You being assigned on this ship, my ship, that

wasn't a coincidence, was it?" If she hadn't been sure before, the truth shone in his eyes as clear as day, as clear as the message she was a fool was stamped on hers. "You purposely got yourself assigned to my ship."

Anger heightened her pitch.

He winced. "It's not like that."

"It's exactly like that. Unless you're denying you arranged this?" She spread out her arm to indicate his being in her sick ward.

"I'm not denying anything."

The way he looked at her made her wonder at just what else he wasn't denying. Surely much more than the reasons behind his arrival on her ship?

"How did you manage to pull off being assigned here? Getting this exact assignment couldn't have been easy. Getting Dr Evans transferred at the last minute, unless that was just a convenient coincidence, which I don't believe. Who owed you a favor? Or maybe it's you who now owes the favor?" She glared at him, battling with the knowledge that he'd gone to a lot of trouble to get assigned to her ship. Why? Even through her blaze of anger that one word shouted front and foremost. "Why? Because you wanted to sleep with me and I turned you down?"

"No."

"Odd," she continued. "For all your faults, I never pictured you as a suck-up, Cole, but you must have been to pull this off."

At least part of her accusations must have hit their target as he didn't say anything. Why had he gone to so much trouble? What had he hoped to gain?

Cole's lips clamped shut. He wouldn't tell her. No matter how many times she asked or how she insisted, he wouldn't tell her how he'd managed to achieve his presence aboard the USS *Benjamin Franklin*. But why not? Surely getting what he wanted was a prize worth bragging about?

Only he hadn't quite gotten what he wanted, had he?

But he'd been on the path. Seducing her into believing in his goodness, making her question what she thought she knew about him, seducing her into forgetting she thought he was a devil in disguise.

Disgusted that she'd let her guard down, that she'd let him in over the past few weeks, Amelia spun, heading toward the medical office, needing to be away from him in the hope of being able to think clearly, of being able to figure out what the truth of him actively pursuing an assignment on her ship implicated.

Why was he here? Doing this? Making her crazy? She wanted to scream over and over, wanted to grab his collar and shake him, make him tell her why he was doing this after he'd so easily walked away from her. Why was he torturing her so doggedly?

She'd just gotten inside the doorway, when Cole grasped her wrist and turned her toward him. Not roughly, but not gently.

"No, Amelia." He denied her escape, his eyes blue fire. "This time you're not running away. We're going to have this out."

What was he talking about? She hadn't run away from him. He'd been the one to ask her to wait for him and then he'd left. Always, Cole had been the one to run.

"There is nothing to have out. Nothing." She

thrust her chin upward. "We're colleagues, working on an aircraft carrier together. As soon as this deployment is finished, our association ends."

"Our association will never end."

Amelia laughed. "Oh, please. Quit being melodramatic. You're acting as if we're star-crossed lovers."

His hold on her arm eased, his fingers feeling more a caress than a restraint when he asked, "Aren't we?"

Nervous tremors crept up her spine. "No. We've barely even kissed."

Kisses she'd relived a hundred times, a thousand times, but still only the kiss the night of the rehearsal dinner and the kiss in her dorm room.

When she'd told him to leave, that she'd waited for him that night and he'd left her, that his window of opportunity had closed, he'd grabbed her much as he just had, pulled her to him, cupped her face and kissed her until she couldn't breathe, until she couldn't tell where she ended and he began, until she'd wanted nothing more than to fall back into her bed with him.

They had fallen back into her bed.

Cole's long body had pressed her into the mattress, moving rhythmically over hers through their clothing, his hands caressing her everywhere at once, as if he'd waited a lifetime to touch her and couldn't quite believe he actually was. Even now she could remember the silky softness of his shiny brown hair, could remember the tangy taste of his mouth, the fervor of his lips on her throat, the hard pressure of his body covering hers.

Amelia gulped, willing the memory to permanently vanish.

"Barely kissed?" He stared into her eyes for long moments, watching, waiting, then his gaze dropped to her mouth. "That's a problem easily remedied."

His head bent, but just as the heat of his breath touched her lips, burned her with more unforgettable memories, she turned her head.

"No." She couldn't do this. Wouldn't do this.

She pulled free, moved away, turning her back to him, gulping air into her starved lungs. "Please leave."

"You don't want me to go."

She turned, forcing herself to laugh in a mocking

way. His eyes were so blue they pierced her. His chest rose and fell in unsteady drags of air. She took all that in, but didn't allow herself to soften. To do so around Cole would be a grave mistake, one he'd pounce upon and devour all that she was.

"Don't tell me what I want," she spat at him in her coldest voice. "You have no idea."

Although maybe he did.

A part of her didn't want him to go. A part of her wanted him to expound on what he'd been telling her, wanted him to explain what had motivated him to show up at her dorm, to maneuver himself into working with her. Had sexual lust driven him to go against his better judgment and search out a woman he'd known would reject him? Did he really believe they were star-crossed lovers or had that only been a smooth line to throw her off balance?

"I know you want me as much as I want you," he countered, not moving from where he stood but looking like he had to force his muscles to remain still. "But you refuse to admit you want me because of loyalty to your sister."

No. She didn't want him.

Much.

"You don't know anything." At least she sounded brave, certain, as if she meant what she said. Inside she quaked. This man held the power to rip her world apart, the same way he had ripped it apart two years ago.

"Tell me I'm wrong, that you don't want me."

She wanted to, but couldn't lie to him. Couldn't lie to herself. Not a moment longer. She did want Cole. More than she'd ever wanted any man.

And it was wrong. Wrong. *Wrong*.

She swallowed the knot tightening her throat. "What I want doesn't matter."

He laughed wryly, without humor. "What you want matters more than anything. You matter. Tell me what you want."

She closed her eyes, praying for strength. "If what I want matters, you'll leave me alone, Cole, because I want you to go."

She heard his sigh, felt his frustration zinging from across the room. His tension wrapped around her like a cloak, willing her toward him, willing her to give in to her desires.

Just when she felt her strength waning, the sensation was gone. *Cole was gone.*

Wondering at her sense of loss when he'd done as she wanted, she opened her eyes to the empty room.

If she weren't a Stockton, tears would have prickled her eyes. But she was a Stockton and those weren't unshed tears blurring her vision because Cole had done exactly as she'd asked.

# CHAPTER EIGHT

HEY, Sis. How are things? Still stationed in the Middle East? Life is busy. The ship was plagued with a virus, but things have calmed down. Only a few new cases this past week.

Amelia dropped her head into her hands.

Oh, God, she sounded like a polite stranger. Just as she'd been sounding in all correspondence with Clara since Cole had arrived on board. She'd told Josie a few weeks ago. She'd even told Robert. They'd both taken the news better than she'd expected but, then, she'd never told them she and Cole had kissed prior to Cole dumping their sister, had never told them about Cole coming to her dorm weeks later.

Just as she hadn't told Clara that her ex was aboard the USS *Benjamin Franklin*.

She had to tell her sister. Now. Today. In this very e-mail.

Pressing her finger on the backspace key, she deleted the entire note and started over.

I've been trying to figure out how to tell you, but Cole is on the USS *Benjamin Franklin*. He is a great surgeon and an asset to the ship, but working with him is difficult for me given the circumstances. I feel my loyalties are torn between you and what's best for my crew. I don't want to forgive him, Clara. I really don't want to, but he does have a way of getting under one's skin, doesn't he? I always cared about Cole, thought he was a wonderful man and doctor. It's so easy to forget how things ended when I'm spending so much time with him, when being with him reminds me of all the things I loved about him.

No, not loved. She deleted the word and typed *adored* instead.

How can I forget how he just abandoned you? Abandoned our family when we loved him as one of our own?

There was that word again. *Love.* They hadn't loved Cole. She hadn't loved him.

"About done?"

Reflexively hitting *Send* before he could read what she'd written, Amelia glanced up at the man standing in the doorway.

Oh, God, she'd just hit *Send*!

All the blood drained from her body to pool in the pit of her stomach.

Would she really have done so if Cole hadn't walked in?

How did he always manage to find her? Not that she was hiding, but he always turned up wherever she was. She'd resigned herself weeks ago to the fact that she wouldn't be able to avoid him. She wasn't even trying to avoid him anymore. What was the point? She was being pursued, stalked by a predator more deadly than any jungle cat.

One that slid on his belly and seduced with his mesmerizing eyes and silver tongue. Just like Eve in the Garden of Eden, Amelia was defenseless against his powers of temptation. Difficult for a Stockton to swallow, but one of their greatest traits was the ability to call an apple an apple and an orange an orange. Stocktons didn't lie, not even to themselves. Especially not to themselves.

She wanted Cole. Had from the beginning. Had he married her sister, she would never have acted on that want, but he hadn't married Clara. Instead, he'd come for her and was biding his time until she was willing to admit she'd been waiting for him to do just that for the past two years.

She'd done what he'd asked. She'd waited for him. Two damn years.

"I was e-mailing my sister," she said perversely, irritated with herself for her weakness.

He didn't physically react, just watched her. "Is everything okay?"

She snorted, too frustrated to hold back what she was truly thinking from him. "Nothing has been okay from the moment you arrived on this ship. No, longer. Nothing has been okay from the moment you walked away from your rehearsal dinner." A pause, as she dragged in an unsteady breath. "How could you have just left? How?"

A pause, a twitch of that perfect set of lips, then, "I'm not leaving you, Amelia. Not this time. I couldn't even if I wanted to."

She inhaled a breath meant to calm her frayed nerves. "Do you want to, Cole? Do you regret manipulating your way onto my ship?"

"No."

Why was she trying to pick a fight? For what purpose? She closed her eyes. "Was there something you needed?"

"Other than you in my bed?"

Amelia clamped her lips closed, her heart pounding at his directness. She should threaten him with sexual harassment, should walk over and slap his handsome face, should do so many things. But all she did was release her pent-up breath.

"Is that what all of this is about?" she asked in a calm voice. Too calm really. "Sex?"

He moved closer, regarded her with speculative eyes. "What do you want this to be about?"

"I don't want this at all, Cole. None of this." She put her hands up in front of her. "I don't want you here, period."

"But you do want me." He wasn't asking a question. He was stating a fact.

She swore softly under her breath in a way that would have her mother going for a bar of mouth-washing soap. "Yes, I want you, but to what purpose?"

"Mutual satisfaction?"

"What makes you so sure you can satisfy me?" she taunted.

His gaze raked over her face in a lazy caress, lowered down her throat, lower, until she'd swear he could see right through her clothes, her skin, to where sweat slicked her body.

"If you'd like proof..."

"No." She shook her head forcibly, moving away from the computer desk, away from where he stood. "I wouldn't like anything from you except to be left alone."

He laughed. "You're like a broken record,

Amelia. Isn't it time you stop protesting so much?"

"Where you're concerned I'll never stop protesting."

"Then the next few months won't be dull, will they?"

How did he do that? Go from seductive devil to laughing like a good ole boy? As if he hadn't just had his proposition turned down flat?

"I thought I'd go up deck and get some fresh air," he said out of the blue, causing her to blink as if she'd missed part of their conversation. "I came to ask if you wanted to come with me."

"Have you heard a word I've said?" she asked incredulously.

"Have you heard a word I've said?" he retorted, arching a brow at her. "I'm not going away, Amelia. Neither am I leaving you. We've tried that, and guess what? Nothing's changed. We need to resolve the unfinished business between us."

"Unfinished business?" she scoffed, knowing she'd lost any offensive hold she'd had. "You mean sex?"

"More than just that but, yes, sex, too." He moved toward her and she got the distinct urge to take a step back. *Defensively.* "But you can rest assured, for the sake of our careers, I can wait until we're at port call." He flashed a smile that couldn't be called anything except bad. "For both our sakes, let's hope you're as disciplined."

Her jaw dropped. "You're a pig."

"I've been called worse."

Why did he keep smiling? Acting as if this was all one big joke? She wanted to hit him!

"Quit being so obtuse!" she chided, frustrated with his lackadaisical smile and attitude.

His lips twitched. "You want to grab a jacket before going up deck?"

Seething, she marched past him and headed up deck before she even realized that's where she was going.

Behind her Cole just laughed. A rich, deep-timbred sound that rocked through her soul.

She should have turned around, gone anywhere other than with him. But maybe fresh air would clear her befuddled brain.

Then again, perhaps only Cole could clear out the confusion he caused.

Thirty minutes later, Amelia and Cole looked out at the dark blue sea. Smoky gray clouds covered the sky and it looked as if it might rain later. They stood opposite an F-14 Tomcat fighter jet, providing them with a shield from prying eyes.

Somehow, he'd gotten her talking about her father. She was never quite sure how Cole did that, got her to talking about herself and her family when she'd had no intention of telling him a thing. He'd even gotten her to discussing her siblings' names.

"Your father is a great man, Amelia Earhart Stockton."

"I don't need you to know that about my father, but thanks." She rolled her eyes at her full name. Her parents had named all their children after individuals they'd admired from history. Well, except Josie. None of the Stockton siblings had ever quite understood why her parents had named their youngest after the lead singer of an all-girl band.

"Growing up with him as a father couldn't have

been easy. I remember Clara saying he…" Cole's voice trailed off.

All righty, then, Amelia thought awkwardly.

"You told her I'm here?"

"Yes."

"What did she say?"

She couldn't tell him that she'd only told her sister earlier that very day in the e-mail she'd sent as he'd entered the room. Besides, why did he want to know what Clara had said? Why did he look so concerned?

She stared out over the horizon. "I'd rather not discuss my sister."

"Don't you think we should?"

She turned to him. "You're kidding, right?"

"Your sister is a wonderful woman."

*La la la.* Amelia mentally stuck her fingers in her ears. She didn't want to hear this. She didn't want to hear Cole extol Clara's virtues.

"But I should never have asked her to marry me," he continued.

*La la la.* She focused on where the sky met the sea, on the wind whipping at her clothes, her face, her hair, on the scent of the ocean.

"Clara was my closest friend, and I mixed that up with other feelings."

"It took you long enough to figure that out. You walked away on the night before your wedding," she pointed out, wincing inside. She hadn't meant to let him draw her into this conversation. She didn't want to have this conversation.

"I'm not going to make excuses for myself, Amelia. What I did was wrong."

"Oh, you're so sanctimonious. Do you want me to get on my knees and bow to your goodness?"

A tic jumped at his jaw. "Tell me you wanted me to marry your sister," he challenged, placing his hands on her upper arms, forcing her to face him. "Tell me you think I should have married her when kissing you that night far exceeded anything I'd ever felt."

"Don't say that."

He stared at her so intently she thrust her chin up.

"I couldn't marry Clara. Marrying Clara would have been the worst thing I could have done to her when I didn't love her the way she deserved to be loved."

"Do you want me to say you're forgiven? That you were a saint to walk away and break her heart?" She glared. "I'm not going to absolve you that way."

"I don't need your absolution," he informed her point-blank, his expression tight. "Clara forgave me years ago."

"Ha," she scoffed. "If you believe that you're a bigger fool than I thought."

He was close. So close. Despite the breeze she could feel the heat coming off him, could feel its pull, could feel the scorch of his fingers on her arms as if he branded her.

"Has anyone ever told you that you are the most stubborn female?"

She lifted her chin another notch, but focused on the slightly crooked slant of his nose rather than meet his eyes. "I'm not stubborn."

"And infuriating," he continued as if she hadn't spoken. "And beautiful. So damned beautiful you make me breathless. I want you, Amelia. More than I've ever wanted anything or anyone, I want *you*."

Shocked out of her anger, her gaze met his and

she instantly realized she'd made a horrible tactical error.

Because the eyes truly were the windows to the soul and Cole had just seen how his words affected her.

His lips came down on hers. Hard.

Automatically, she bit him. Hard.

He swore against her mouth, but didn't step back, just kept on kissing her, willing to take whatever punishment she doled out. Only he gentled his lips against hers, swept his tongue into her mouth with slow thrusts, leaving himself vulnerable to any retribution she opted to wield against him.

She should bite him again.

She really should.

But he tasted so good, felt so good. She'd waited two long years to feel this good again. She leaned against him, her palms flattening against the width of his chest, and relaxed, giving free access to her mouth.

He held her, his hands pressing her tightly to him, his body hard against hers. But his kisses remained gentle, exploring, a mating dance meant to seduce her into bowing to his whims.

She hated him. And yet...she didn't.

He lifted his head, breathed raggedly against her mouth, stared into her eyes with a wildness in his she'd never witnessed. "You make me crazy, Amelia. Certifiably crazy."

Breathless, she strove for her usual cool. "You don't exactly do much for my intelligence either, Einstein."

He laughed softly, resting his forehead against hers. "That shouldn't have happened."

Something inside her plummeted at his words.

"Not here." He raked his fingers through his hair. "Not where someone could have seen us."

She bit the inside of her lower lip in relief, and frustration. He was right, but...

"Don't look at me like that, Amelia. I want you too much. At the moment I want to carry you off to the closest bunk and our careers be damned if it means I can have you."

"Oh." Was that pleasure curling in her belly?

Why did his admission make her feel so…desirable? Wanton? Sexy?

"Yes, 'Oh,'" he mimicked, and gave her a look so intense she had to take a steadying breath. A look so full of desire and passion and pure unadulterated lust that she could only stare at him in wonder. "You're safe for now but, come port call, you're mine. No more games, no more pretenses, you are mine."

# CHAPTER NINE

A TOTAL of three months had passed since Cole's arrival aboard the USS *Benjamin Franklin*. Currently, the aircraft carrier was docked at the Changi naval base in Singapore. Cole had spent the morning working with one of the ship's chaplains in humanitarian efforts in the city. He suspected Amelia had, too, but he hadn't seen her. Probably intentionally.

Since their kiss, she'd become wary, watching, studying him. The looks she'd stolen weren't hostile, more resigned. As if she'd accepted that eventually the sparks between them would ignite and burn them both.

*You are mine.* Where had that he-man statement come from? He wasn't the knock-them-out-drag-them-by-their-hair kind of man. Never had been. Then again, no woman had ever affected him the way Amelia did.

She really did make him a little crazy. Very crazy.

But all of that would change. Soon. Tonight?

Several of the crew had planned to meet up at a bar that was a regular hangout of military personnel in Singapore. The bar was just a few streets from the port and one of many that catered to the thousands of soldiers that made port call at the only Asian port deep channeled enough to accommodate an aircraft carrier. Cole and a couple of the other medical crew who'd volunteered with the chaplain walked together at the end of their charity stint.

The streets were crowded, filled with exotic noises and smells. Fish markets, delicacies from street vendors, and Chinese, Malaysian and various ethnic restaurants tempted his nostrils. Modern skyscrapers gleamed high above the streets, glistening against the setting sun and providing a spectacular high-tech backdrop that spoke well of Singapore's prosperous world-class port.

Even without the upbeat rhythm of the city, an excitement filled the air. Physical excitement.

Cole and Peyton had signed out as liberty buddies that morning and were checked into a hotel the ship had arranged. In separate rooms.

Inland, physical release was fair game and happened in excess. Thousands of young soldiers with money burning holes in their pockets and a few days to drink, party and be merry before returning to their life aboard ship.

With sexual relations forbidden on ship, port call often served as a sexual smorgasbord either between crew members or with locals.

Cole had never indulged in that particular aspect of port call. Drinking to excess and deafening his pals with poorly sung karaoke renditions, yes. Meaningless sex just didn't do it for him. Even before his assignment aboard the USS *Benjamin Franklin*, a long, long time had passed since he'd last been with a woman.

He'd been okay with that. Then. Now he could honestly say he was more sexually wound up than at any point during his life. But he had no plans to pick up a strange woman in a bar. Meaningless sex still didn't appeal. He planned to find Amelia and finally make good on his promise.

*You are mine.*

Amelia was going to be his.

If she wasn't at the bar, he wouldn't stay long, would go in search of her and he'd find her. She was checked into the same hotel as he was. All the medical staff were. Suzie was her liberty buddy and had no qualms in letting Cole know that their room was on the same floor as his, only a few doors down.

His sole purpose for the next two days was to spend as much time with Amelia as possible. Preferably in his bed.

When he and the group he was with entered the low-lit bar, Cole skimmed the crowd, taking in soldiers mixed in with locals. He recognized numerous USS *Benjamin Franklin* crew and nodded acknowledgment to several who called out to him, but he declined their offers to join them. He was on a mission.

"Who are you looking for?" Peyton asked, casting a sly glance Cole's way. "A particular female doctor perhaps?"

Cole didn't answer his colleague.

"It's no secret you've got the hots for her. You planning a little port call party for two?"

He scowled at his liberty buddy. "Watch what you say."

Peyton held up his hands. "No offense meant, man. I just figured she was who you were looking for. It's obvious there's something between the two of you."

Then Cole saw her. Every corpuscle in his body contracted into a tight ball.

*She was his.*

Her hair was down. Lying softly across her bare shoulders, the tips trailed between her shoulder blades. She wore an exotic sundress of reds, greens and golds that made her eyes shimmer like molten liquid. Never had her eyes seemed so erotic, so luminous. Possibly because of the makeup brushed across her lids, her cheeks, the gloss puckering her all too kissable lips, but he suspected the look had more to do with an internal beacon she emitted. One every ounce of testosterone within him responded to.

Sitting with a group of nurses, corpsman, Suzie and the ship's other medical officer, she had a brightly colored drink in front of her and a happy look on her face.

A little too happy a look.

She laughed at something someone said, leaned over and laid her head on Suzie's shoulder for a brief second in a very non-Amelia type gesture. Way too relaxed, way too touchy.

Cole frowned. How long had she been at the bar?

Her gaze lifted, clashed with his, sent conflicting signals that said *Come and get me if you think you're man enough* and *Go away, you're not wanted* at the exact same time. No woman had ever sent stronger mixed signals.

Cole chose to go with the first option. He was definitely man enough and he definitely wanted to come and get her. Still, he wouldn't rush. He'd found her. He'd take his time, savor the building sexual momentum and make his move when he was ready.

Of that, neither of them had any doubt. Was that why she drank? To lower her desperately clung-to guard? To have something to blame come morning light?

He didn't like the idea, but there was nothing he could do about it other than make sure she was sober by the time they got back to the hotel. No way would their first time be with her drunk. She'd come to him of her own free will.

Peyton and the others Cole had entered with joined Amelia's group, pushing up another table and chairs.

Amelia's lips parted and her gaze dared him to join them.

Shooting her a smile that revealed nothing and yet promised everything, he crossed to the bar, was greeted by more colleagues and ordered a beer.

He swapped stories with a friend he hadn't seen in over a year that was serving on a battleship in their battle group. He bought a beer for a crew member, turned down three offers to dance from women he didn't know and only occasionally glanced toward Amelia.

Each time he did, he found her watching him. And tonight, for the first time, she didn't bother to look away when he caught her.

Her big brown eyes boring into him, tracing

over each feature as if trying to figure him out, to figure out why he hadn't tossed her over his shoulders and carried her back to his hotel room. If only she knew how desperately he wanted to do that, yet that same desperation was what held him back. He wouldn't lose control. To do that would just be foolish.

A captain, full of himself, presented himself to her, strutting like an inebriated peacock.

"Dance with me, pretty lady," he slurred, bowing in grand gesture and drawing a couple of chuckles from others at the table.

Amelia's gaze slid from Cole to the man. Slowly, she shook her head back and forth, declining his request.

He didn't leave, though, instead cajoling her to change her mind, flashing smiles and phony compliments. The room was too noisy for Cole to make out exactly what he said, but he'd have to be blind to miss Amelia's reaction to the flirting and her subsequent reconsideration of the man's request.

*No.*

Cole left his bar stool, cleared a straight path

to Amelia's table, his gaze never leaving his quarry.

Distracted by the man, she hadn't noticed his approach, but her tablemates had. Suzie smiled, giving him a "what took you so long" look. Sitting to Amelia's right, Tracy elbowed her.

"Hey!" Amelia protested, glancing away from the captain to the nurse. "What was that for?"

Her brows lifted expressively, the woman gestured toward Cole. He didn't move, just stood, feet spread wide, arms at his sides, ready for whatever she threw at him.

"Oh." Her full lips rounded in surprise.

Or feigned surprise at any rate.

He'd just been had. She'd had no intention of dancing with the man, just of *making him* jealous, making him come to her. She'd played him.

"Cole," she purred, her eyes full of wicked delight.

"Yes. Cole." *Don't play games with me, Amelia. Not tonight. Not ever.* "Sorry I took so long," he said for the benefit of the captain unhappily observing his interruption and looking imbibed enough to mistakenly think he could stake a claim despite Cole's arrival. He shot the man a "she's mine, back off" glare, then returned his attention to Amelia. "I got caught up talking to an old friend, but I'm here now." He held out his hand to her. "Let's dance."

Amelia melted into Cole's arms, laying her cheek against the soft material of his cotton-blend shirt. He wore some funky button-down with jeans. Seeing him in civilian clothes should make her think of when they'd been in school. Perhaps it did. But rather than remember, she was assailed with new thoughts.

For years she'd blamed him for what had happened, never considering that perhaps Cole hadn't wanted the attraction between them any more than she had.

Perhaps he still didn't.

Maybe he was as trapped by the chemistry between them as she was. Not wanting the attraction, but unable to resist it. That she understood all too well. Hadn't she barely slept the past several nights, guilty with the knowledge she'd soon be at port call, would soon embrace her feelings for Cole?

Her arms draped loosely around his neck, toying at his nape. He'd had his hair cut at some point during the day, but the sun-streaked locks were just as soft as she remembered.

He smelled so good. Spice and soap and musky male. The scent of him intoxicated her more than the cocktails she'd been drinking in the hope of drowning out her guilt.

Sure, Clara's e-mails said she didn't want Amelia to hold the past against Cole, that Cole was a good man, that they'd just not been meant to be. Her sister was trying to make things easier, trying to lessen Amelia's burden. If only her sister knew.

Yet like a silly moth flitting into a light, she couldn't stop the events from unfolding, couldn't even try. Every instinct she had drew her to Cole, closer and closer until she'd burn.

His hands pressed against the bare skin of her back, his body swaying with hers to the music. "I like your dress."

"Thank you." She'd bought the multicolored

dress earlier that day and liked the way the material clung to her body, almost making her appear to have curves. Had she worn the dress because the style made her feel feminine? Less of a soldier and more of a woman?

"I like what's in it better," he breathed close to her ear.

Puh-leeze. She may have been drinking, but she hadn't completely lost her senses. Not yet.

"Don't use cheesy lines on me."

"Why? Won't they work? Looked like the lines I interrupted were working quite effectively." The way his jaw worked when he said it belied the easy tone of his words.

"What's wrong, Cole? Jealous?"

"Of another man holding you?" he asked, tensing against her, his hands holding her a bit tighter, his jaw practically clenched. "Hell, yes."

"You don't own me, Cole. I can dance with whomever I please, whenever I please."

Some ground rules needed to be established. Like that no matter what happened between them, she was her own woman. She'd do as she pleased, when she pleased, and with whom she pleased. If he didn't like that, he could get over himself.

"I know," he agreed, looking smug and like he saw right through her, like he knew just why she protested and found it cute. Cute! "Which is why you're dancing with me, Amelia. You please me very much."

He'd twisted her words, which should infuriate her. Instead, warmth spread, settling low in her belly. "I do?"

"Don't play games," he warned in a low growl that sent shivers across her skin. "We're beyond games. You know you please me, that you're all I think about, kissing you, touching you, tasting you. I want you so much I ache."

The warmth erupted into all-out explosive heat at the intensity with which he spoke.

He was right. No more game playing.

Biting her lower lip, giving herself up to the inevitable, she met his gaze. "I ache, too."

"I know." He sighed, his palms flattening against her back, holding her against him. "I know you do. It's just the way things are between us. A constant, undeniable ache neither of us can fight."

"I'm tired of fighting, Cole. So tired." She rubbed her cheek against the strong wall of his chest, realizing that she *was* tired. Tired of having to be strong, tired of fighting what she was feeling, tired of the guilt, the frustration, the anger, the pain, the desire of wanting him, the wondering why he'd asked her to wait then left. She was tired of all of it and just wanted to lean on Cole, to soak in his confident strength, if only for a short while.

He kissed the top of her hair, breathed in her scent. "We both are, sweetheart. For the next two days, we don't have to fight anything, least of all each other."

Whatever resistance she might have been able to muster vanished. She gave herself over to the music playing between them, moving in beat to the tune, going wherever Cole led regardless of the consequences that were sure to follow.

Too bad that rather than leaving, he led her back to the table where their friends were, because escaping became almost impossible.

Where had the bottle of Jack Daniel's come from, anyway?

Peyton poured a measured amount into the glasses of everyone at the table. On a high from her dance with Cole, Amelia upended her shot glass and lifted it to the cheers of her tablemates.

They were drinking like the sailors they were.

Round after round, they drank, laughed, recounted tales of shared experiences, pranks pulled and personal blunders.

Amelia sat next to Cole, plastered to his side, their hands locked beneath the privacy of the table, although they probably weren't fooling a soul.

She laughed, shifted. Their hands slid across her lap. Cole tensed next to her with the awareness that his hand lay across her leg with only a thin scrap of silk between them. An awareness they both felt.

An awareness that was burning her up from the inside out, waiting, burning, building, growing hotter and hotter until she felt she was about to burst into uncontrollable flames.

Without letting go of her hand, he gently raked his fingers over the material, bunching the cloth higher, slowly exposing the flesh beneath. Other than a quick glance his way, she didn't externally acknowledge what he did, just carried on the conversation without skipping a beat, much as he did. Beneath the table, a whole different conversation was taking place.

One without words. One that didn't need words.

Cole's fingers did the talking, praising the toned lines of her thighs, telling her how much he wanted her, telling her all the things he planned to do to her before the sun came up.

They spoke volumes to each other, conveying all the things words couldn't.

Even when she was at the point of squirming in her seat, he didn't move to the damp juncture of her thighs. She wanted him. Desperately wanted him to touch her there. But he didn't. Just traced delicate lines along her inner thighs to almost the brink of where she craved him most.

Over and over he drew the path, circling, toying, rubbing over her skin in teasing little movements, his hand dragging hers along for each erotic stroke. His fingers touched her, but he also played her own fingers against her flesh, guiding each teasing touch. Each movement tugging her insides out until she reached the point she fully expected her skin to retract.

What was he doing? How could he stand it? Oh, God, she couldn't take much more without climbing into his lap.

Or dragging him under the table.

She glanced at him, her brow furrowing at how relaxed he looked, at how little he seemed affected by his tantalizing caresses. Her gaze settled on the rapid little beat pounding at his neck and she felt the beginnings of a smile.

Mr Hot Shot Doctor could act as if he were immune to what he was doing, but that jumping carotid pulse told a different story. One that emboldened Amelia.

Wiggling her hand free, she began an exploration of her own. One that involved her hand on his rock-hard thigh. Seconds later she discovered his thigh wasn't the only thing rock hard about his body. Had he just groaned or had she imagined that guttural sound?

No longer able to fake an interest in the conversation going on around them, she lifted her glass to her lips with her free hand and drank deeply. Her other hand remained on him. On the very male part of him that just touching had her panties going damp.

Through his pants, she cupped him, taking slow measure of his girth through the material. Impressive. Wow.

He swallowed, forgot what he was saying and laughed roughly. "Somebody pour me another drink. I need another."

"That's funny," Amelia said low next to him, quite enjoying herself. "I'd say you need something else entirely."

He turned to her and stopped. He swallowed. Hard.

"Never mind," he told no one in particular, his gaze not leaving Amelia's. "I've had enough anyway. I'm going to head back to the hotel. Anyone else ready to go?"

"Already? It's too early to turn in, man," Peyton

denied, glancing at his watch. "The night is barely getting started."

A perverse part of Amelia wanted to deny Cole, to stay here and torture him, to make him beg her to come with him. But to do that would torture herself.

She'd been tortured two years too long already.

Although she liked the idea of Cole begging. Begging her to open her mouth to his kisses. Begging her to touch him. Begging her to strip off her clothes so he could—

"Amelia?"

She blinked, having missed whatever else had been said.

"Are you ready to go? You're looking a little flushed."

Oh, she was definitely feeling a little flushed. Otherwise she wouldn't be running her hands over the skirt of her dress, smoothing the material over her thighs and then sliding out of her chair. Her legs practically wobbled beneath her.

"Yes." She glanced around the table, but didn't meet any of her colleagues' eyes. "Thanks for a fun evening. I'm going to turn in so I'll be fresh for sightseeing tomorrow."

Not a single one of them were fooled by her and Cole's dialogue. She knew that. Cole knew that. They all knew that. Still, she smiled, waved goodbye and kept her head high.

Until she stumbled.

Cole caught her elbow, steadied her.

"Oh, to hell with this," he mumbled, wrapping his arm around her shoulder despite the fact they were still in the bar and in view of their friends and colleagues.

His arm felt too good to push away. Besides, now that she'd stood up she felt more than a little light-headed. She wasn't sure she could walk out of the bar without falling flat on her face if Cole let her go.

So she leaned against him, letting him guide her out of the bar and into a taxi. When the door closed, she turned to him, looking up, waiting for him to do what they'd been working toward all evening.

But he didn't.

Instead of kissing her, taking her back to that

warm happy place she'd discovered on the deck of the USS *Benjamin Franklin* when he'd kissed her, he took her hands in his, clasped them tight and shook his head.

"Cole?" she asked, confused.

"I can't," he bit out between gritted teeth.

"You can't?" She blinked. Didn't he want to kiss her? Wasn't that why he'd rushed them out of the bar? Wasn't he going to take her back to her hotel room and fill this ache deep within her? Was he going to make her beg?

With the way she felt, she would.

"If I touch you, we'll end up making out in the backseat of a taxi," he explained, his expression pained. "As much as I want to kiss you, I want more than desperate gropes in the backseat of a car."

"Desperate gropes in the backseat of a car aren't so bad," she muttered, both pleased and disappointed that he was restraining himself when she so desperately wanted to be kissed.

"It is when you want a lot more," he clarified, giving her a look that seared to her very core, a look that said once he started touching her, he wouldn't quit come hell or high water. "And have waited two years."

Gulping in anticipation, she leaned forward, getting the taxi driver's attention. "Could you drive faster, please?"

# CHAPTER TEN

AMELIA woke with a bad taste in her mouth. A very bad taste.

Oh, God, had something crawled into her mouth and died?

Slowly she became aware of other body malfunctions. Like the steel drums playing inside her skull and the way her brain had swollen to three times its normal size. God, but she had a headache.

And what was that smell?

Not bad. Actually, quite wonderful. She breathed in deeper. Spicy. Musky. Yummy. Mmm, definitely male.

Male?

Amelia prised a heavy eyelid open and didn't know whether to wince or lick her lips.

Cole lay next to her, his bare chest easily qualifying as the most beautiful male flesh she'd ever laid eyes on. And not just her eyes were on him.

Oh, no, even in her sleep she'd reached out and touched him.

Her hand lay across his abdomen. Low on his abdomen. His flat, chiseled, hard abdomen that made her fingers tingle.

She licked her lips.

Then winced.

She jerked her hand back before she did something else. Like move lower to discover just what the sheet riding low on his narrow hips hid.

Or had she already discovered that?

Grimacing, she took stock of the fact she lay in a hotel room bed. She glanced around. His hotel room bed. She wore nothing but her underwear. Thank goodness she'd worn pretty matching blue silk numbers. But why did she still have them on?

Surely she hadn't taken time to get dressed afterwards?

Afterwards. Had she and Cole made love?

Maybe if her head didn't hurt so badly she could

remember. Somewhere amidst the pounding was the knowledge she desperately needed to recall.

What did it say if they'd finally had sex and she couldn't even remember? That she was having to rack her brain in hopes of recapturing the moments?

It said she'd drunk way too much after night after night of not sleeping well from stress.

She'd known what was going to happen between them, known Cole would pursue her, would take what he wanted. What they both wanted. But she'd felt guilty knowing she and Cole would make love, that before the sun came up she'd have given herself fully to him and taken every morsel of affection he'd give to her.

She'd drunk her guilt away, but she had still wanted to remember!

She squeezed her eyes closed, willing the memories to come to her.

She thought back, remembered being in the cab, remembered walking through the elaborate hotel lobby, going up in the elevator. Cole had run the back of his hand along her neck, forcing every hair on her body to stand at attention. He'd leaned in, blown hot breath against her nape, his lips so close yet not actually touching her sensitized flesh.

Her nipples had puckered. Her knees had knocked. The elevator door had slid open. Cole's hand had moved low on her back. He'd guided her two doors down past her room into his own, pushed her inside and kissed her.

No, not kissed. He had *devoured* her mouth.

She remembered his lips on hers, remembered thinking he was the most marvelous kisser, him moving lower, kissing her throat, telling her how beautiful she was as his hands and mouth moved lower, and then…and then…nothing.

Opening her eyes, she glanced toward Cole, studied his sleeping perfection. From the top of his gorgeous head to where the narrow ribbon of hair disappeared under the sheet, he was perfection. Pure male perfection.

Had she had sex with that male perfection?

"Morning, beautiful."

Her gaze shot to his. Sleep gave the blue of his eyes a lazy hue, but she didn't mistake that hue for lack of complete awareness. After all, he knew what had happened between them.

Why was he *smiling*?

Panic rose up her throat. Disgust? Regret? Shame? She couldn't stand not knowing.

"What happened last night?"

He rolled onto his side, regarded her with an indulgent expression. "You don't remember?"

She wished she'd jumped up, brushed her teeth, combed her hair and washed her face before he'd awakened. This would be a lot easier if she didn't feel so grungy.

"Obviously sex with you isn't that memorable," she quipped, determined not to make a bigger fool of herself than she already had.

"Obviously," he surprised her by agreeing, laughter dancing in his eyes. "Only we didn't have sex."

Surprise number two.

"We didn't have sex?" Had her voice just squeaked? *They were practically naked in bed together.*

His lips twisted wryly. "When we have sex, I'd

prefer you to be awake rather than asleep in my arms."

She'd slept in his arms?

"Yes."

Had she asked that out loud? Since he was grinning at her and he'd answered, she obviously had. Brilliant.

The corner of his mouth lifted higher. "You have the sexiest little snore when you're drunk."

"I wasn't drunk." She didn't even believe herself, neither did she want to tell him about her poor sleep habits as of late, so she added, "Much."

Scooting up on his pillow, he laughed.

"Okay, maybe I was a little tipsy." Dragging her gaze back from where the sheet had inched farther down on his hips, barely covering the very male part of him that she'd apparently not seen the night before. Her own state of undress became more of an issue and she tugged on the sheet, tucking the edges beneath her arms to hold the material snugly around her. "I should go."

The laughter in his gaze flickered and he let out a long sigh. "Are we back to that?"

She thought about what he was asking, what he

was really wanting to know. Now that she wasn't under an alcoholic haze, was he once again the enemy?

She couldn't find the words to answer, didn't know how to answer. Could she get past what had happened? Had she already? Was that why she was with him? Because at some point over the past few weeks she'd stopped thinking of him as the bad guy and started seeing him as the attractive man she'd always been crazy about.

"Amelia." No longer looking amused, he raked his fingers through his short hair. "I'm not going to apologize for wanting you."

"I didn't ask you to apologize," she huffed, crossing her arms over her chest.

"But you regret being here with me? That we spent the night together?"

She tugged the sheet more tightly around her. "Nothing happened. You said so yourself."

"I didn't say that nothing happened." Two wonderfully sculpted shoulders shrugged. "Just that we didn't have sex."

"But—" She glared at him, feeling at a distinct

disadvantage that she didn't remember what they'd done. Or not done. "What exactly happened?"

A smile once again pulled at the corner of his mouth. "One of the highlights was when you begged me to make love to you."

She gasped, wanting to call him a liar, to tell him he was remembering wrong.

"And?" Had he said no? She couldn't believe it. And if he had refused her, what were they doing in bed together?

"You stripped off your dress in the worst—and yet definitely the best," he added as if recalling a particular memory, "striptease I've ever been privileged to witness."

"Seen a lot of stripteases, have you?" she bit out, wondering how big a fool she'd been and vowing to never drink alcohol ever again. Never ever, *ever* again.

"Not really, but last night's was spectacular on many counts."

"But not so spectacular that we actually had sex."

Was she upset that the striptease she couldn't

remember had been a dud? Pride. Had to be wounded pride.

"Make no mistake, Amelia, if you hadn't fallen asleep, I would have made love to you until you couldn't see straight." His gaze bored into hers, pinning her to the bed. "Until you couldn't do anything except whimper my name in ecstasy."

She'd have liked him to have made love to her like that. Over and over until her eyes rolled back in her head and she arched off the bed and...

"You have no idea how *frustrated* I was when I realized you weren't faking."

His all-too-real exasperation got to her and her spirits lifted a tad. They may not have had sex, but not from a lack of Cole having wanted to. Good.

"Most men don't want women to be faking in bed," she said, giving what she hoped was a sexy look of challenge. Something that might have been more effective if her hair wasn't wild about her head, and who knew what her smudged slept-in makeup looked like?

"Tell me about it." He snorted, taking measure of how she'd begun to relax. "Now what, Amelia?

You didn't answer me. Do I need to buy a bottle of Jack Daniel's and ply you with whiskey to convince you to spend the day with me?"

Whether she'd meant to or not, she couldn't keep the smile from her face. Despite the way things had ended the night before, Cole wanted to spend the day with her. In bed?

"You'd better tell me what you want to convince me to do before I answer."

Good point. One Cole would think had a simple answer. But nothing about his relationship with this woman was simple and hadn't been from the moment they'd met.

Last night, she'd begged him to make love to her, to kiss her all over. Hell, he'd been on his way, his hands on her bare waist with her lying back on the bed. He'd been trailing kisses over her abdomen, tasting the salty goodness of her skin, working his way lower.

Then she'd snored.

*Snored.*

Even with as frustrated as he'd felt, he'd laughed out loud.

"Amelia?" he'd asked, moving to her side, trying to rouse her.

"Cole?" she'd muttered, rolling to her side and curling against him without ever opening her eyes.

"I'm here, babe." He'd wrapped his arms around her, knowing he wouldn't be making love to her. Not tonight. But soon.

Her face had nuzzled against him. "I waited for you, Cole. I waited and waited and you left. Please don't leave me again. I couldn't bear it."

Her sleepy request had pricked him, made him feel protective of her sleepy vulnerability, made him horribly guilty for past mistakes.

"I promise, Amelia. I won't leave you." He hadn't wanted to leave her that first time, but another promise, to Clara, had demanded he do just that.

He had held her all night, waking several times amazed to find her really with him, curled against his body spoon fashion.

Not the way he'd planned to spend his first night in bed with Amelia, but not bad. Holding her, waking to her chocolate eyes was quite nice.

The fact that her eyes begged him to push her back on the mattress and take the decision of how they'd spend the day out of her hands, to not give her a choice so she wouldn't have to feel guilty for her actions stole that nice feeling, though.

She didn't want to take responsibility for what happened between them.

Not last night. Not today. Possibly never.

Which meant nothing could happen between them.

*Hell.*

He wasn't a nice guy. It shouldn't matter what her reasons were. She wanted him, was giving him a come-hither look, was visually asking him to make love to her right at this moment.

He wanted to make love to her. Which made his rolling onto his back and staring up at the ceiling in frustration all the more crazy.

"I thought we could go sightseeing."

He didn't have to look to know she wore a surprised expression. She was stunned. He was feeling a little stunned, too. She'd been flirting with him, waiting for him to take advantage of the fact they were in bed together, practically naked, and that he could easily seduce her.

Her vulnerability when she'd asked him not to leave her flashed through his mind again. Amelia was too important to jump the gun. Yes, he wanted her, but he wanted her to want him just as much, for her to be willing to admit that she wanted him rather than feel guilty about their lovemaking. This time there could be no guilt, no bad blood between them. They'd make love because it was what they both wanted, no recriminations.

"There's an animal park not far from here," he rushed on, needing to step away from his making-love thoughts. "We could take a taxi over, spend the morning there, grab some lunch, then wander through Little India, check out the shops and eat dinner at whatever restaurant takes our fancy."

Mouth slightly slack, she stared at him as if she didn't know whether to hit him or kiss him. She did neither. She flopped back on the mattress, stared up at the ceiling along with him. The two of them must look a sight, both scantily clad, lying on their backs, staring up at a pristine white ceiling, frustration emanating from their bodies.

"Okay," she said slowly, not sounding sure of her voice. "I'll go to an animal park with you, and I've always wanted to check out Little India, so that would be good, too." Her lower lip pouted just a tad. "Maybe you won't put me to sleep again."

Did she have any idea how beautiful she was? How much he wanted to make love to her at this exact moment? But what was happening between them was too fragile to cloud the issues with sex. What issues he didn't want to cloud he wasn't sure, just that he'd made the right choice, however difficult, in delaying their mutual gratification.

It was simply a delay.

"If you go to sleep again," he threatened in his most menacing tone, "I'll toss you to the tigers and return to the ship alone."

"Hey." She reached out and punched his arm, then re-crossed her arms over her chest.

"Of course," he continued, unfazed, "that snore of yours might scare the stripes off them."

"I thought you said my snore was cute and

little?" she shot back, without moving from where she lay, staring straight up. Her voice held a teasing quality that he could quite easily get addicted to.

He leaned over, but made no play to touch her, just moved into her line of vision, studying the way her hair lay about her head in tangles, how her makeup smudged beneath her eyes, how her lips pouted with the need to be kissed. A thousand sunsets couldn't compare to her beauty. "I called it sexy and little, but I might have exaggerated."

"You think?" She giggled and something shifted inside him and he wondered if he was too late, if perhaps issues were already so cloudy that eventually a storm would hit no matter how carefully he proceeded.

"I don't even want to think of all the ways I humiliated myself last night," she continued.

"Then don't. Last night doesn't matter. Today's a new day."

"You're right. It is a new day. Let's get started." With that, she darted from the bed, presenting him with the most delectable view of her bottom in tiny royal blue silk panties as she disappeared into the bathroom.

Later that day and for the dozenth time, Amelia wondered what was she doing and, just as she'd done each time, she shoved the thought aside.

She had the right to be with Cole. He was single. She was single. They were healthy, consenting adults going into this with their eyes wide open. The past didn't matter.

She didn't really buy her mental pep talk, but she deceived herself that she did. Otherwise she wouldn't be able to justify how her hand rested in Cole's as it had done most of the day. Neither would she be able to justify how they'd talked, laughed, enjoyed each other's company. Like lovers.

For crying out loud, she'd let him feed her bites of his lunch. The scrumptious pieces of fish they'd bought from a street vendor had practically melted in her mouth.

Just as she was melting in Cole's hands like butter in a hot frying pan and she was enjoying every sizzle.

"Come on," he urged, pulling her into a shop doorway.

She'd been too lost in her thoughts to pay attention to where they were, but looking around the luxurious, tranquil setting she knew.

His eyes sparkled with a happiness she hadn't seen in...years. Happiness like that they'd once always shared. Together. Because being together had made her happy and, looking back, she realized that being together had made Cole happy, too. He'd always smiled for her. A real, deep-down-from-the-heart smile.

No one's smile had ever lit up her world the way the man grinning at her did. In that moment just how much she'd missed him hit her. *Oh, Cole.*

"No one can come to Asia without getting a massage."

"Oh?" She arched a brow, intrigued by him having brought her there. "Is that in the travel guide?"

"Word for word. I memorized it when you went back to your room this morning to shower." He winked, talked to the Malaysian woman who greeted them, then handed Amelia over to her care. "Go with her. You'll be glad you did."

A massage was tempting, but not as tempting as the man whose hand she already missed. She hesitated only a moment. "What about you?"

"What about me?"

"Are you going to get a massage, too?"

His lips curved at the corners. "You think I need relaxing?"

"Actually, you look more relaxed than I recall seeing you in years."

His gaze tangled with hers, cocooning her in blue warmth. "Don't let the outside fool you. I'm so wound up on the inside I could snap in two."

Figuring he was referring to sexual tension, she grimaced, took a deep breath and told him the truth. "I really am sorry I fell asleep. I wanted to make love to you, Cole."

He studied her a moment then shook his head, surprising her yet again. "I can't believe I'm saying this, but I'm not sorry. We needed today, just you and me, spending time together, remembering what was good between us."

Yeah, maybe they had. But inebriated sex would

have been easy to explain to her conscience. Tonight, when they made love, she wouldn't have anything to blame except the attraction between them. A terrifying thought.

Time for another mental shove. Clearing her thoughts, she lifted her chin in a play of deviance. "I'll only have a massage if you have one, too."

He laughed. "You're going to twist my arm?"

"If that's what it takes," she insisted, but knew the smile on her face disarmed her threat.

"Fine," he agreed, sounding more amused than anything. "We'll get a massage together."

He turned back to the woman who worked there, told her what he wanted, and she nodded her dark head.

A massage together? As in both of them on the table? How did that work? Instantly visions of her naked body lying on top of his flashed through her mind. Um, yes, that could work very nicely.

Cole took her hand and led her through a maze of exotic scents and colors, following the Malaysian woman into a room just for the two of them.

Twenty minutes later, Amelia was in heaven.

She lay on a massage table of sorts, a masseur rubbing and kneading every muscle in her body.

"I heard that moan," Cole said from opposite her, the head of his table a mere meter from hers with them lying in a straight line, feet outward. "You like?"

"I like," she admitted, wondering at herself for lying naked except the sheet covering her in a room with Cole also naked except for the thin cotton sheet covering his delectable backside. Not that she'd looked. Much. A young girl worked on him, sculpting his muscles between her nimble fingers in an almost exact mimic of how the young Chinese man rubbed Amelia.

They lay in silence except for the mood music playing in the background and the sounds of their breathing. Sweet incense burned in the four corners of the room. Peace, tranquility, happiness and love, they'd been told.

"I can't believe we've been naked in the same room twice and haven't slept together yet."

"I'll just bet." Amelia laughed at Cole's bemused comment. "Must be some kind of record for a man like you."

"Must be," he agreed, but only halfheartedly, his words slightly muffled from where he lay facedown on his massage table. "I'm not as active as you think."

Amelia laughed. "Don't tell me that, Cole. I heard about all the nurses you went through after you and Clara broke up."

"I was trying to forget." His admission was low, self-derisive, as if he had lots of regrets.

"My sister?"

His answer came out clearer than before. "You."

She lifted her head, saw that his was also raised, looking at her. She stared straight into his eyes, was pretty sure she was drowning in their blue depths. "Did it work?"

After a few moments, he said, "I'm here, aren't I?"

There was no justification for the satisfaction that filled her. None whatsoever. But satisfaction did fill her.

Cole had sought her because he'd wanted her.

Other women hadn't done, hadn't satisfied him. Would she be able to?

"I'm not as experienced as you," she admitted. Lowering her head back into the face rest, she wondered how they could carry on a conversation with the two people giving them massages listening in. Maybe it was the anonymity of being halfway around the world. Maybe it was because the masseuse and masseur were foreign and it was easy to pretend they couldn't understand English, despite knowing that most everyone in Singapore spoke the language.

"I'm not some Casanova." He sounded a little irked. "I've been selective about who I've become involved with. There haven't been that many women in my life."

Closing her eyes, she tried to give herself over to the warm oils being massaged into her flesh. This was supposed to be relaxing. This was relaxing. Only the conversation made her feel tense, worried her. Why was she being so open with him? Why was she telling him the things she was?

"It's not that I'm a virgin." For instance, that

was one of those things she really shouldn't have said out loud. She really hadn't needed to divulge that tidbit. "But a woman doesn't want to think she doesn't have enough experience to satisfy her man either."

"Are you calling me your man?" he asked slowly.

Heat burned her face, but to deny his question would be foolish. They'd slept together the night before. Literally slept together. Today they'd held hands, indulged in conversation and prolonged foreplay through long looks that revealed too much. Tonight, they'd make love.

"Is that okay?" She squeezed her eyes shut, holding her breath as she waited for his response. Praying he'd say the right thing.

"Yes, Amelia, that's more than okay." He lay there a moment then declared, "I'm going to buy a bale of whatever they're burning. Peace, tranquility, happiness and love."

"Do what?" Still smiling, Amelia craned her neck to glance at him. He lay with his chin propped up on his hands, watching her. The young woman kneaded his calf muscles.

He smiled at her. "Obviously, whatever we're breathing has made you mellow since you're talking out of your head."

She returned his smile. "Right or wrong, I do know what I'm saying."

More wrong than right, she knew, but wrong sure did feel right in regard to the man lying a few feet from her.

"I hope so, Amelia. I really hope so."

After that, they were silent for the remainder of their massages. No matter how wonderful the therapeutic oils and massage, she couldn't bring herself to completely relax. Not when her mind raced with events to come and not knowing quite how she would deal with the aftermath of those events.

Then again, how did one prepare for heartbreak?

And one was coming on as surely as she was a Stockton.

# CHAPTER ELEVEN

AMELIA went to her room after she and Cole arrived back at the hotel. Suzie hadn't been there and it didn't look as if her bed had been slept in any more than Amelia's had. The damp towel hanging on the back of the bathroom door said her friend had returned and changed for the evening already, though.

Amelia showered, changed into a strapless dress she'd bought from a shop that afternoon and carefully put on makeup and styled her hair. She'd forgone a bra, her mostly flat chest not requiring much anyway, and slipped on a pair of barely there red silk panties that rested high on her hips.

"You look amazing," Cole greeted her when she opened her hotel room door following his knock.

"Thanks." She smiled, running her gaze over him. "You look pretty great yourself."

He did. At the same shop she'd bought her dress, she'd found a pirate shirt and teased him into buying it. She hadn't really expected him to wear the swirls of white material, but he was and he looked fabulous. All he was missing was a gold hoop in his ear and a sword. The shirt's material accentuated the width of his shoulders, the girth of his chest, the narrowness of his waist. Women would be lining up to walk the plank. She'd be at the front of the line.

"Let's just stay in."

Cole's suggestion echoed what was running through her mind. She might have grasped hold of his shirt and tugged him into her room if another hotel room door hadn't opened. Tracy stepped out into the hallway wearing a dynamite red dress.

"Hey," she called, immediately spotting them. "You two look great. We missed you today at the MRW tour out to the bird sanctuary and downtown."

"We decided to check out the city on our own."

Smiling, Tracy nodded at their clothes. "Looks like you found some good shops."

"A few."

Another door opened and Peyton stepped into the hallway, a blonde Amelia didn't recognize hanging on his arm. He invited them to a nearby bar. "We're all meeting at eight for drinking, dancing and lots of bad karaoke."

Cole's gaze met Amelia's. She saw longing to say no in his eyes, saw that he really did want to push her back into her hotel room and watch a repeat striptease, that the last thing he wanted was their colleagues as an audience to the emotions bouncing back and forth between them tonight because too much was happening between them for there to be witnesses.

But he said, "Sounds like fun. Are we walking or taking a cab?"

At the bar, Amelia limited herself to one drink, sipping slowly. Tonight, she wanted to be sober, to stay awake, to remember every detail of what happened between her and Cole. She laughed at all the right times, spoke at all the right times, but her mind danced ahead, to what the night would bring, to what making love with Cole would be like.

Heaven, she decided. Making love with him would be out of this world. Had to be since just thinking about making love with him had her on the brink of orgasm.

"You're not getting sleepy, are you?" Cole leaned in near her ear. His breath tickled, sending shivers over her flesh.

Lifting her glass and taking a small sip, she shook her head. "No way. I have plans for tonight."

"Oh?" He sounded intrigued, his breath warm, moist against her ear. "What kind of plans?"

"Ones involving being captured by a pirate and staying awake long into the night."

He glanced down at his shirt and frowned. "I'm no pirate, Amelia, and I won't capture you. Either you'll come to me of your own free will or nothing will happen. Not tonight. Not ever. That's how it has to be between us. No games. No lies. Just you and me together because it's what we both want."

Amelia blinked.

He'd pursued her. She'd just told him a fantasy. And he'd changed tactics? He wanted her to come to him? Did he want her to beg again, too? But knowing how she held a grudge for past actions, maybe he was right to insist on her being the one to initiate their physical relationship.

Actually, she knew he was.

She didn't like him for doing so, but she understood.

He was giving her no wiggle room to blame him for seducing her or to say that she hadn't wanted whatever happened between them.

No room for guilt afterwards. Either she made the conscious decision to make love with him or they didn't make love. The choice was hers.

Whether he meant to or not, he was seducing her, though.

With his eyes, his smiles, his little "accidental" touches. And then there was his leg rubbing against hers.

Unlike the night before, he hadn't attempted to push up her dress and touch her thigh, hadn't stroked her flesh into a tortured mass of nerves that cried for release. No, all he was doing was pressing his leg next to hers. That was enough to fry her brain cells.

"I will come to you, Cole. Tonight." Admitting as much wasn't easy, but with so many other issues between them, communication was of paramount importance. "But I'm not going to beg, do you hear?"

"I hear." Oblivious to the others at the table, he brushed a lock of hair off her cheek, tucking the strand behind her ear. "I'll be the one begging tonight, Amelia."

His husky promise caught her off guard, melted her to her seat.

"I want you, Cole." Heat flushed her cheeks. "I'm not going to make you beg."

"But I will," he whispered. "I'll beg for mercy, because you wield power over who I am and I want you that much. More."

His words sank in and she tried them on for size.

Maybe there was a reason they couldn't stay away from each other despite all the reasons they should. Maybe he'd fallen for her just as she'd fallen for him.

Even as she thought it, she knew she could never trust Cole, that at some point he'd walk away from her just as he'd done two years ago. But for the moment it was nice to bask in the glow of the magic of the promise in his eyes, in the fact that for now she was who he wanted, and they were together.

"I want to go back to the hotel," she admitted, not willing to wait another second. Afraid that if she did, reality would sink in and rob her of the warm feelings rushing through her.

His brow shot up. "Now?"

She nodded. "Let's go."

They said their goodbyes to their colleagues, most of whom were enthralled in a tale Richard was telling with great animation. Amelia didn't have a clue what he was talking about, didn't care. All that mattered was the burning desire in Cole's eyes.

Desire for her.

His palm pressed against her low back possessively, he led her across the dance floor toward the front of the bar so they could make their exit.

Unfortunately they were only halfway across the crowded room when a fight broke out.

Cole cursed, shaking his head in frustration. "What's Peyton done this time?"

Amelia's head whipped around to see the nurse anesthetist's fist smash into a man's face. She winced at the impact, at the way the man's head snapped back. Peyton reared back to hit him again. Others joined the fight, some in an attempt to break up the argument, others to get in hits of their own.

Amelia sighed. Fights weren't uncommon at port call. Actually, they were quite the norm. Several thousand soldiers barely out of their teens, some still in their teens, let loose with money in their pockets, too much pent-up testosterone and too much booze wasn't a good thing under the best of circumstances.

But Peyton wasn't a kid. He was a highly trained anesthetist and one of their own. Cole wouldn't leave him. Neither could she without making sure he was okay and not in need of medical attention once the fight ended. Plus, several of the men involved in the fight were USS *Benjamin Franklin* crewmen.

Warning her to step back, Cole bustled his way toward where a cluster of men scuffled. Knowing she could hold her own in any fight, she followed him. By the time they reached the group, the fight had broken up. A corpsman's face was bleeding from a cut on his cheek. Another's nose bled profusely. Peyton rubbed his knuckles. A few others would sport bruises of various shapes and sizes come morning, but no one seemed to have suffered any critical injuries. Getting a couple of towels and ice from a bartender, Amelia went to the bleeding soldiers.

"Here." She handed the towel to the one with the bleeding nose. "Pinch your nostrils tightly together."

Using her fingers and nose, she demonstrated the proper technique. When he looked as if he might lose his balance, she shoved a bar stool toward him. "Sit down, pinch your nose like I showed you and don't attempt to move until I tell you it's okay."

He did as ordered.

Cole was checking Peyton's hand so Amelia turned to the soldier with the cut on his face. The slash wasn't so deep or jagged that it required an emergency room visit, not really, but he would need a few stitches for the area to properly heal with minimal scarring.

Which meant she or Cole, probably both, would be heading back to the ship to attend to the injured crew's needs.

So much for their night of sexual excess.

A bus carried the somber group back to the ship. Although Cole's gaze met hers a time or two, they'd not talked more than to give a rundown of casualties.

On the bus, he sat with the soldier needing stitches and Amelia had ended up in a seat with Peyton, a plastic bag filled with melting ice plopped over his swollen hand.

"That's going to smart in the morning. Why did you hit that man, anyway?"

Peyton shrugged, not saying more. He didn't need to. The blonde she'd seen coming out of his room earlier now sat with the soldier whose nose had been broken by Peyton's punch. She oohed and aahed over the soldier like a mother hen. Had they had a lovers' spat and the woman had used Peyton? Or had Peyton taken advantage? Who knew?

"You should reset his nose without any pain-killers."

Amelia frowned at her friend. "You're just saying that because he got the girl."

"He can have the girl," Peyton scoffed. "I got the only thing I wanted from her this afternoon."

Amelia winced at his crudeness. "Men are so gross."

"Yeah? That wasn't the impression I got when you were looking at my boy earlier."

"Your boy?"

"You know who I'm talking about."

"You really should be quiet before you end up in another brawl, Peyton," she warned.

He laughed. "Talking about Cole get you hot and bothered?"

Half grinning, she narrowed her eyes. "Makes me fighting mad. Be quiet before it's your nose having to be reset without painkillers."

* * *

Amelia set the nasal bone back into place as best she could, and left the corpsman in a bay with the blonde watching over him.

A radiology technician had shot a few films of Peyton's hand and he had a non-displaced fracture of his middle metacarpal. He wouldn't need surgery, but he'd be sore for several days.

Cole was in bay two with the soldier with the cut face. He set up a suture tray.

"Here we are again," she teased when she scrubbed her hands and took over the task for him. "I'll finish setting this up. You scrub and get gloved."

Sending her a wry smile, he did as she asked, explaining to the man sitting on the table what he planned to do in step-by-step detail.

"I'm going to disinfect the cut and surrounding skin first. Then I'll numb the area with anesthetic. Once you're numb, I'm going to use skin glue to close the laceration."

"Glue?" the man questioned.

"It's special glue made for closing certain types of cuts. When used appropriately there's less scarring. Plus, there won't be a need for you to return to have sutures removed."

The soldier shrugged. "Ain't never had to return to no doctor to have stitches took out. Been doing it myself since I was a kid."

"Had a lot of accidents over the years?"

"A few," the man admitted, grinning. "A few fights, too."

When he was ready, Amelia held the edges of the wound perfectly closed while Cole ran the glue applicator over the area, creating a purplish clear coat over the cut and sealing the wound.

When they were finished, it was too late to return to the hotel.

"Not exactly the way we envisioned spending the night together," she mused when they stood outside her bunkroom door.

"We're starting a pattern here that I can't say I like," he teased, bringing her hand to his mouth and kissing each of her fingers.

"Agreed." She laughed, feeling like a kid on her first date.

"I wish I could stay with you tonight, Amelia."

He squeezed her hand, held on tightly. "I would if I could."

"Maybe next time." But even as she said it, she wanted him to tell her to hell with rules, to hell with everything but them. Which was crazy. She didn't really want him to tell her that. They had too much to lose to risk if they were caught.

"Maybe."

She looked up into his eyes, wondering if he'd at least sneak a good-night kiss. But he straightened to his full height, gave a shake of his head.

"Good night, Amelia."

"Good night, Cole." Reluctantly, she watched him turn and go, disappointed and hoping they hadn't missed their window of opportunity forever.

Okay, so maybe covertly blowing a kiss at Cole when no one was looking wasn't exactly playing fair, or even mature, but Amelia couldn't resist it.

Since Singapore they'd walked a fine line between flirting and keeping enough distance to not end both their careers. With every day that passed it was getting a little more difficult to recall the reasons why her career mattered so much more than being with Cole.

Giving a wry shake of his head, he slyly winked back from across the sick ward. The flash of desire she'd seen in his eyes, the possessiveness, caused happiness to blossom inside her. Pure, deep-down happiness.

The only blight on her happiness was the fact that, despite the looks, the stolen touches, the fact they both wanted each other desperately, they'd played by the rules and hadn't slept together yet. Somehow.

Which was good, because if they had done there would be hell to pay. They couldn't, she knew they couldn't, but, oh, how she wanted to.

God, she wanted him, wasn't sure how much more she could stand.

"Dr Stanley," she said in her most professional voice, flashing her most innocent expression, "could I see you in the medical office for a few moments, please? I need your advice on the last patient I saw."

Another spark shone in those blue eyes. This one caused her stomach to somersault.

"I'll be right there, Dr Stockton."

He was, closing the door behind him because he'd known. Known she needed to touch him.

"We can't do this," he told her even as he pulled her to him.

"I know." She smiled against his mouth, flattening her palms against his chest, relishing the strength she found there. "I just needed to touch you."

"Amelia," he groaned. "You're killing me."

"I'm sorry." But she wasn't, and they both knew it. "I just look at you and have…" she stared at his mouth, bunched the material of his shirt beneath her fingers "…needs."

His lips twitched. "What kind of needs?"

"This kind." She tilted her pelvis against him, circled her arms around his neck. "The kind that makes me not be able to think about anything but how much I want you, Cole Stanley. How I ache with wanting you."

Another groan escaped him just as his mouth covered hers.

Amelia kissed him back, loving how he felt, how he tasted, how he poured every ounce of his being into kissing her.

"I want you so badly, Amelia."

She knew he did. She could feel just how badly digging into her belly.

"This is torture," he continued. "Being so close, wanting you, knowing you want me, too, and yet not being able to make love to you."

She knew just what he meant and nodded. "Sweet torture."

"There's nothing sweet about how I feel about you."

"How do you feel about me?" She hadn't meant her question to be a serious one, just a teasing one meant to elicit more comments about his sexual frustration and desire for her. Cole's answer was serious, though.

"Haven't you figured that out by now, Amelia?" He cupped her face. "You're all I think about, all I want. You are my everything."

"You're my everything, too, Cole." Unable to look away from the truth in his eyes, Amelia stroked her fingers across his precious face, worrying that she was so head over heels for Cole she'd never resurface if the ship tipped. "Now shut up and kiss me again before I go see my next patient."

He burst out laughing, hugged her tightly to him. "God, I love you."

When he kissed her, Amelia almost believed that he really meant it.

# CHAPTER TWELVE

HAVING decided she wasn't going to sleep no matter how long she lay in bed, Amelia snuck out of her room, careful not to wake Suzie.

She'd go to the medical office, catch up on reports, check her e-mails, anything other than just lie in bed longing to be with Cole.

The weeks had passed by much more quickly than she would have liked. Weeks she spent every possible moment with Cole. Talking, laughing, stealing kisses, touches, sharing long looks, sharing longing for much more. By sheer determination, they'd held on to enough willpower to not go beyond kissing and hot touches.

Very quickly their deployment was coming to an end and they'd return to the naval base in San Diego. She'd likely go to work at a mainland hospital or perhaps even at a combat support hospital overseas. Who knew where Cole would end up?

Odds weren't that they'd be anywhere near each other. Possibly not even on the same continent.

Then what? Would their romance come to an end? Would they be able to steal a few days together at the base and finally make love before being reassigned?

Make love.

Because whether she'd wanted to or not, she'd fallen for Cole.

Okay, so if she was honest with herself, she'd admit she'd never stopped wanting him. He listened to her, took her needs into consideration, sometimes knowing what she needed more than she'd known herself.

Amelia paused in the medical office doorway, startled to see Cole at the desk. What was he doing?

Glancing past him to the lit computer screen, she could see his e-mail account opened. Ah, checking e-mails. The same as what she'd come to do.

Instead, she'd found the man she wanted. For all time.

Which scared her. How could she want Cole when he'd eventually leave her? But what if he didn't? What if he really did love her? He'd said he did that one night. Okay, so it had only been that once and it had come out on a laugh, but that hadn't stopped her heart from going thumpity-thump-thump.

Just as it was going thumpity-thump-thump right now. She hadn't counted on seeing him again tonight, hadn't counted on getting to steal more kisses.

God, she wanted more than just stolen kisses. She wanted hours and hours of Cole all to herself, no rules, no recriminations, no fear of dishonorable discharge.

But stolen kisses would do. For now. She smiled, planning to walk up behind him and cover his eyes with her hands and have him guess who. Maybe she'd just lean over and kiss his nape.

She noted the tension emanating off him.

He studied the screen, his shoulders a bit slumped, the angle of his head low.

Had he gotten bad news? His mother was the only family he'd ever talked about and she'd died when he'd been a teen. Suddenly worried that something was wrong and wanting to comfort him if needed, she stepped into the room.

"Hey, stranger," she said, smiling to hide the nervous flutters in her belly. "What's up?"

He straightened in his chair, taking on a stiff appearance, as if guilty of some dastardly deed. "Everything's fine."

He sounded distant, almost as if he didn't want her there. Something was definitely wrong. She stepped farther into the room, closed the heavy door behind her and moved into his line of sight so she could see his face.

"You're sure?" She dropped into a chair near his.

He leaned back in his chair, glanced toward the computer screen. "Nothing's wrong. Just have a few things on my mind."

She understood. She had a few things on her mind, too, all of which centered on him and how they were running out of time together. Soon they'd have to give whatever was between them a name, make decisions about whether or not they were going to see each other once their stint on the USS *Benjamin Franklin* ended.

"You seemed tense when I came in."

He scowled. "There's not anything wrong, Amelia. Go back to your room."

Right. Because he always sounded angry with her, always didn't look her in the eyes when he talked to her, always told her to go to her room.

Enough was enough. There was definitely something wrong and she had a pretty good idea what it was.

"You're shutting me out, aren't you?"

His jaw worked in a slow rotation and he raked his fingers through his hair. "I'm not shutting you out. Let it go. I'm really not up for this tonight."

She put her hands on her hips, not willing to walk away. "It feels as if you're shutting me out, and I don't like it."

What was wrong with him? She'd never seen him like this. So ragged. So rough. So raw.

"God, you just don't know what you do to me, do you?"

Her breath catching, she met his gaze, held it. "Tell me."

He laughed ironically. "You make me not care about anything except you, Amelia, about making love to you and holding you and being able to sleep with you in my arms."

Okay, not a bad start to their conversation so why did he look so upset? Angry almost?

"I'd say turnabout was fair play, wouldn't you? I care a lot about you, too, Cole. I want those same things, think about them when I'm lying in my bunk, unable to sleep because I want you there with me." She met his gaze. "Like tonight when I ached so badly to be near you that I had to escape out of my room."

His throat worked, his eyes closed and his fingers gripped the chair arm so tightly they blanched white. "I'm hanging by a thread here, Amelia. You should go."

He was pushing her away. As much as that hurt, she wouldn't let him push her away without giving her an explanation. "Why would I go?"

The blueness of his eyes threatened to engulf her. She fought to keep from glancing away.

"I want things I shouldn't want on board this ship." His words came out as a low growl.

Proverbial lights clicked on above Amelia's head. "I should stay away from you because of the ship rules? That's why you're telling me to go away?"

Looking tired, frustrated, he nodded. "We've both worked too hard to risk our careers for a night of passion."

He was trying to put distance between them to protect their careers. Admirable. Logical. She took a deep breath. "How about six nights of passion? That's what we have left."

His brow arched. "You think that would be enough?"

"You tell me. What's the past six months been about?"

He shrugged. "You. Me. Sex."

"Sex?" She laughed, hoping she didn't sound hysterical. No longer able to sit, she paced across the small room. "We've not had sex."

"You think I haven't noticed that?"

She twisted to glare at him. "It's our lack of sex that's the problem?"

He ran his fingers through his hair again. "Our lack of sex is a huge problem."

"Then why did you get assigned to the USS *Benjamin Franklin*, Cole? If not to sleep with me? You don't have to chase a woman halfway around the world to get laid, Cole. We both know that. Explain so I can understand why you came here and turned my world upside down."

Apparently unable to sit a moment longer either, he stood, his back to the desk. A tic jumped at the corner of his mouth. "You know why."

"We both know you could have had me months ago if sex was all you wanted." She hated admitting that, but it was true. Just a few touches and all protests would have gone up in smoke. "Tell me why you're here, Cole."

He didn't say anything, just stood seeming to consider his next words. She couldn't stand the silence. Not a moment longer.

"What made you pull favors and board my ship, Cole? Why did you pursue me and torture me by being everywhere I was? Was this all some sick joke to you? Mess with Clara's little sister's head and heart?"

Red splashed across his cheeks and his fingers clenched at his sides. "Why I'm here has nothing to do with Clara, and you know it."

"Do I?" But staring straight into those beautiful blue eyes, she did know. Cole cared about her. More than just wanting to get her into bed.

Despite the way her heart hammered in her chest, she pressed forward.

"I think you care more about me than you're willing to admit, Cole. I think that's why you're here, why you got assigned to the USS *Benjamin Franklin*—to be near me."

"God, you're direct."

He hadn't denied her claim. Oh, God, he hadn't denied what she'd said. He did care. She clung to that belief, clung to a lifetime of being taught to go after what she wanted and not let anything stand in her way. "I'm a Stockton."

"And Stocktons always get what they want?"

Had he read her mind? Laughing wryly, she shook her head. "Apparently not. If we did, I'd have made love to you every day and night since Singapore."

His gaze shifted from hers, then back. The

pulse at his throat jumped wildly. Had her words brought him back to the night at the hotel, before she'd fallen asleep? Back to the following night when they'd been headed to the hotel to consummate the fire burning through them?

"You don't know what you're saying." He raked all his fingers through his hair, glanced toward the computer screen as if the monitor would give him the answers he needed. "You're better off that we haven't done anything."

"Do you really believe that? I don't." She took a few steps toward him. "What I do believe is that for the rest of my life I'm going to regret not making love to you while we have the chance." In her heart, she knew it was true. If she didn't seize the moment, if she was a coward and didn't embrace her feelings for Cole, she would always have regrets.

"This is crazy." He laughed, as if by doing so he was giving validation to his claim.

"It is crazy…" insanely, wonderfully crazy "…but it's true. We have one week left, Cole. Less."

"And?"

"I want to spend the remaining time with you."

"We've been spending time together." At her pointed look, he winced. "Amelia—"

"Don't Amelia me," she interrupted. "I know what I want." She leaned forward, cupped his face. "Kiss me, Cole."

His jaw tightened beneath her fingertips. "I can't kiss you. Not tonight. Not when we're both at our wit's end with need."

Part of her registered that he spoke sense, that she should heed his warning. But another, bigger part feared never knowing what it felt like to make love to him.

"You kissed me up on the steel beach prior to Singapore," she reminded him. "And a hundred times since."

"I shouldn't have. Anything that happens between us needs to wait until we're in San Diego. No more kisses until then, Amelia."

He made sense, yet she wasn't satisfied with his answer. Wasn't satisfied period.

"Who knows what's going to happen once we dock? We'll be given new assignments and may never see each other again." She couldn't imagine her life without seeing him and knew in her heart that she'd find a way to him, would ensure their paths crossed in the future. "Kiss me, Cole." When he didn't move, she sighed in frustration. "Fine, you just stand there and I'll do all the work myself."

She placed her lips against his. She half expected him to push her away, to tell her she was crazy again.

He didn't.

"What are you doing to me?" he groaned. He kissed her back, pulled her to him and wrapped his arms around her, cradling her next to him. "Don't you realize I've fought to keep from doing this for fear of what it would lead to? That I won't risk your career? Won't risk hurting you in any way? We can't do this. I can't do this. I'm not strong enough to kiss you and walk away, Amelia. Not tonight. I want more."

His anguished words were all it took for love to burst free in her chest, leaving no doubt in her mind exactly how she felt about him, leaving no doubt about exactly what she wanted. God bless him, he thought pulling away from her was the right thing to do.

It wasn't. Not by a long shot. Not for her. Not for him.

"I don't want you to walk away, Cole. I want you. I feel as if I've always wanted you." She sank against him, opened her heart and soul to his plundering.

With an agonized moan, he did plunder.

With his mouth, his teeth, his hands. Amelia plundered right back. She kissed him with all her heart, all her soul, with all the passion she'd felt for him for years. She touched his face, the strong lines of his neck, his broad shoulders, the sinewy contours of his back.

He touched her, too. With his hands. With his mouth. His lips were everywhere. Her throat, her clavicle, her breasts.

"Cole," she breathed, pulling him back to her mouth. "Oh, please."

She didn't want him to stop, ever.

She ran her hands down the front of his uniform, moved her hips against his hard groin.

She wanted him so much.

She hadn't planned this. She hadn't come looking for him, but now that she was kissing Cole, she didn't want to stop.

Not ever.

She tugged his shirt from his pants and slid her fingers under the material to the sculpted flesh.

At her touch, his stomach sucked in, his breath catching. "Amelia," he said on a warning note.

A warning she had no intention of heeding.

Her hands caressed his body, moved low, cupping him through his pants as his mouth ravaged hers in a conquering of spirits.

It wasn't enough, didn't satisfy the ache within her, and she fumbled for his zipper.

He broke the kiss, his head lifting as he stared down at her, his eyes a hazy, drugged blue. "Amelia?"

Worried that he meant to push her away, she kissed him, pressing as close as she could. She didn't want him to stop. She wanted him to love her. To really love her.

The way she loved him.

With all her heart and all her soul.

That's what she wanted from him. Everything.

"You're sure this is what you want?" he asked, his voice husky and raw.

For answer she parted the fly of his pants, shucking the material down just enough to run her hands greedily over him. "What do you think?"

"I think you're driving me crazy."

"Good, then we'll go together." She freed him, stroking her fingers along the length of him. "Love me, Cole. Please love me right now."

Even if just for this moment. Even if just for this short glimpse of time.

They'd both lost their minds, Cole thought. That could be the only explanation for Amelia coming to him.

Yes, he'd known she wanted him, just as he'd always wanted her. But to hear her openly admit how much she wanted him made him feel as if he could propel the USS *Benjamin Franklin* with the energy bursting free within him.

Her talented fingers closed around him, circling

where he throbbed. He bit back a groan of unmitigated pleasure. A groan of sheer torture.

They couldn't do this.

"I don't have a condom, Amelia. We have to stop." While he still had enough wits to stop. He was close, so close to being beyond reason, beyond anything except the scent of her arousal, the feel of her desire enveloping them both in its seductive cocoon.

Looking dazed, she smiled at him, making him want to smash his mouth against hers in a savage kiss that would leave them breathless and clamoring for more.

"I'm on the birth control shot to stop my menstrual cycle." She named the brand. "I won't get pregnant, and I'm clean, if that's what you're worried about."

Although that was something he should have been worried about with as many diseases as were out there, that hadn't been what concerned him most. What worried him was his need for a barrier between their bodies, between his heart and hers. He definitely needed that.

And more.

Because she made him lose reason and he needed to stop this while he still could.

She blinked at him, her eyes soft melted-chocolate pools full of desire, her lips swollen from his kisses, her fingers circling him, not too tight, not too loose. Just right. Oh, hell.

"Are you?"

Was he what? He couldn't think with her hands on him.

"Yes." He wasn't sure if his response was in answer to her question or to her hands gliding along him.

"Good," she breathed against his mouth, kissing him.

Cole hadn't lost control during sex since...he couldn't remember ever having lost control. But if someone had forced him to describe what happened next, he'd have to say he'd lost control.

He certainly wasn't been under control when he jerked her pants down or when he flipped her around and pressed her against the wall. Control was nowhere in the building when, his hands holding hers above her head, he thrust into her wet softness.

There had been nothing controlled about the way he drove into her, letting go of her hands to rest his on either side of her head. Or in the way his mouth lowered to the curve of her neck, kissing, sucking, knowing he was leaving a mark and, despite the fact he'd never been one to leave marks on women, reveling in the fact Amelia would bear a sign of their passion. He wanted her marked as his. Forever.

*Idiot.*

When she convulsed against him, whimpering in pleasure, he lost it. Lost everything. Vision. Speech. Hearing. His *mind.*

He definitely lost that.

Black bursts blinded him. The taste of her throat muted him. Her pleasured cries deafened him. The quivers of her orgasm stole all semblance of sanity and he thrust hard, coming deep inside her, dropping his forehead to the top of her head.

Sweat soaked his skin, heat burned his body.

Shame burned his soul.

He'd taken Amelia like an animal in heat.

She turned, faced him, looked up at him with a smile on her contented face. "Wow," she whispered, wrapping her arms around his neck and kissing the corner of his mouth. "Wow. Wow. Wow."

Wow was right. It had been good. Great. But what he'd just done to her hadn't been making love. That had been sex.

Good old-fashioned up-against-the-wall sex for the sake of sating physical need. Amelia deserved so much better. He'd wanted to give her better. How could he have treated her this way? She'd never believe she meant more to him than just sex now.

He'd just used her and she was smiling at him as if he'd done her the greatest favor.

What had he done?

Someone knocked on the door. The handle moved. Amelia's smile disappeared, her eyes widening as she scrambled to restore her clothing. Cole did his pants up in record speed, trying not to look guilty as the door swung open.

Oh, hell. Someone could have walked in on them. To have been caught like teens would have been a horrible humiliation without the added issues of what getting caught on board ship would mean.

How could he have compromised Amelia this way? What was wrong with him?

"Hey," Peyton said, stepping into the room, then pausing, his astute eyes taking in where Amelia still stood next to the wall, Cole stood a few feet away. The room probably smelled of sex.

The nurse anesthetist paused, clearly deducing what had been going on as his gaze met Cole's. *What the hell?* his expression asked. *Have you lost your mind? You can be sent packing for this.*

Cole kept his expression blank, battling with a flurry of emotions. He couldn't put Peyton in the position of having to keep secrets. Neither could he put Amelia in the position of being dishonorably discharged. Hell, he'd already put her in that position. Had put his roommate in that position. *Idiot.*

"I, uh, came to…" Peyton paused, eyed where Cole stepped protectively in front of Amelia. "Actually, I forgot something. I'll just go take care of that." He gave Cole a meaningful look. "You coming?"

Cole tried not to wince at the question. "In a minute."

Peyton frowned. "You sure? Someone might get the wrong impression with you two shut up in here."

Or get the right impression.

"I need to close my e-mail account," Cole said, gesturing toward the computer screen. "I was checking my e-mails."

"Right, checking your e-mails," Peyton said, his forehead wrinkling. "You want me to wait for you?"

His friend was trying to save his rear end, to say that he'd be right on the other side of the door so nothing else could happen, so they wouldn't risk their careers for a few moments of pleasure.

Too late.

He glanced toward Amelia, took in her disheveled appearance, her kiss-bruised lips, the contentment yet appeal in her eyes. She didn't want him to go, not until they'd talked.

Need for reassurance shone in her chocolate

depths and stupidly he wanted nothing more than to wrap his arms around her and give her that reassurance. To lift her into his arms, carry her to somewhere private and spend the night loving every inch of her body. The right way rather than against a wall.

They had to stay away from each other or a repeat would happen.

He couldn't allow a repeat.

Not when doing so would lead to Amelia hating him yet again.

If they got caught it would mean her career. In a heated moment, she might be willing to take that risk, but she'd grow to hate him if he dishonored her, destroyed her military career.

And his career right along with hers.

Where Amelia was concerned, he had a short fuse. Short? Knowing what being inside her felt like, he didn't have a fuse. He looked at her and wanted to self-detonate.

Which meant for both their sakes he had to establish distance between them right here and now before they destroyed their careers. Before he destroyed the way she felt about him beyond repair.

"Yes," he told Peyton, moving to the computer, "I think you'd better wait."

"Cole." Amelia moved toward him, but he held up his hand. She cast a cautious glance toward Peyton who in turn raised his brow at Cole.

"You mentioned you'd forgotten something?" Cole reminded his friend, knowing Amelia wouldn't let him just slink away like the fool he was. No, she'd make him confront what happened. Better if that happened without an audience.

Peyton's lips pursed. "I'll be just down the hallway."

He nodded his understanding. Peyton intended to play big brother and make sure Cole played by the rules. Where had his friend been twenty minutes ago when he'd needed a rush of sanity?

When Peyton stepped out of the room, Amelia took another step toward him, but Cole held up his hand to ward her off. The pain in her eyes sucker punched him.

But he had to do the right thing by Amelia. Even

if he hadn't moments ago. Especially because he hadn't moments ago.

They'd almost been caught. Had it been someone other than Peyton they'd be in trouble already. He cared too much for her to do that to her. He shouldn't have put her in this position to begin with. But he couldn't resist her if she actively pursued him. Not when she was everything he wanted wrapped into the most amazing package. Saying to hell with rules and spending the next few days buried inside her was too tempting.

He'd do whatever was necessary to protect her, even if he was protecting her from him, from herself.

Unable to meet her eyes, he turned.

He never should have come on board. Never should have risked hurting her. What would her father say?

John Stockton had made him promise he wouldn't do anything to put Amelia at risk.

If discovered, the Admiral would have Cole's head on a platter.

But that wasn't the worst of it. No, the worst

would be living with the guilt of knowing he'd hurt someone so precious to him. Again.

"That was too close," he began. "You need to stay away from me, Amelia. This can never happen again. It shouldn't have happened. I didn't want it to happen. Not like this."

She stared at him as if he'd lost his mind. "You're the one who pulled strings to get commissioned on my ship. You chased me until I couldn't deny what I felt for you any longer. Stay away from you?" Glaring, she snorted. "Is that what you told my sister when you broke her heart, too?"

"I didn't break her heart."

"You broke off the engagement. Of course you broke her heart."

Cole took a deep breath and told Amelia what he should have told her two years ago, but had felt honor bound not to. "I wasn't the one who broke things off."

Face tingling with disbelief, stomach roiling with nausea at the regret stamped on Cole's face,

Amelia bit into her lower lip. "Clara called off the wedding?"

His shoulders sagged. With relief? Hurt?

She knew about hurt. She'd just had the best sexual experience of her life end in disaster. Yes, it could have been worse. Peyton could have walked in on them five minutes earlier. They could be facing charges for not abiding by the rules.

"Yes, she did."

Oh, God. Clara had called off their wedding? Not Cole? Amelia's brain tried to wrap around his words, around the implications, and couldn't.

"Why would she do that? She was devastated. She couldn't have been the one to call things off." Tears stung her eyes, but she'd die before she'd let a single drop fall. Dear sweet heaven. Clara broke things off with Cole? *Why would any sane woman not want to marry him?*

She must have seen their kiss. Must have been hurt by such a betrayal. Amelia's eyes stung. Why hadn't her sister said anything? Two years and Clara had never spoken of what she'd seen, had given Cole a glowing recommendation just a few weeks ago. Had her sister been giving her permission to love Cole?

"After you and I kissed," Cole began, "I went to find her, planning to confess, but she called off the wedding before I could say anything."

"Why didn't you say anything?" She wanted to hit him, hard. He hadn't been the one to break things off. Clara had. And he'd left. Left! "You asked me to wait for you and then you left me." She pushed against his chest, anger and hurt competing in her belly. "Why would you do that?"

"Clara asked me to leave."

He said it so matter-of-factly that she stared incredulously at him. "You couldn't have taken the time to talk to me? To tell me the truth?"

"No."

She let his answer digest. "What about when you came to my dorm? Why didn't you tell me then? If I'd known Clara had been the one to break things off..."

"What would knowing have changed, Amelia? Would you have welcomed me that night?"

Would she have? Probably not on the night he'd come to her dorm. She'd been too hurt by that point. "Had you come to me on the night of the rehearsal, had you told me everything then, I would have welcomed you."

"I couldn't tell you. Clara didn't want your father to know the truth." He glanced away, paused, then added, "For any of you to know the truth."

Amelia tried to ignore the fact that he'd let Clara's wants come between them, tried to understand, but she wasn't sure she did. "Why are you telling me now?"

"Clara released me from my promise."

Clara released him… Amelia's gaze landed on the computer screen, registered who the e-mail pulled up was from. A fist gripped her trachea and refused to let go. "You've been e-mailing my sister?"

Was that guilt on his face? Oh, she couldn't breathe, couldn't think, couldn't keep her hands from shaking.

"I hadn't talked to her in months, but she e-mailed me after port call in Singapore. We've been in contact since."

Cole hadn't left her sister. Cole hadn't called off his wedding. Clara had. Her brain cells fired in a million different directions. "Why did you just make love to me?"

"That wasn't making love, Amelia. That was sex, and it shouldn't have happened. Not with so much at stake."

Not making love. Sex. Shouldn't have happened. Her vision blurred. "Are you in love with my sister?"

He rubbed his hands across his face, looked torn, then his gaze lifted to hers and he took a deep breath. "I've always loved Clara. I always will love her, but that isn't what this is about, and you know it. This is about you and me and what's between us."

Amelia couldn't take any more, couldn't deal with all the emotions barreling through her. She'd given her heart to Cole, accepted that she loved him, had given her body to him freely, and he'd used her.

She felt dirty. Horribly, horribly dirty. Used. She was stupid. Very, very stupid. She'd been nothing more than an itch Cole had wanted to scratch. Part of her mind acknowledged that didn't make sense, that he'd gone to too much trouble for just sex, but heartache blinded her to reason.

She called him every vile name she could think of, balling her hands into fists and pounding them against his chest.

Rather than stop her, he took her abuse, letting her vent her anger until she realized she was accomplishing nothing. Her halfhearted hits didn't hurt Cole. Her rashly flung insults didn't pierce his cold heart. He didn't care. He'd gotten what he'd wanted from her.

"Clara dumped you and your damaged male pride demanded retribution. You knew how I felt about you and you used me, didn't you, Cole? Used me to get back at my sister."

He didn't deny her claim and great pain sliced through her, reminding her of all the reasons she'd vowed never to love in the first place.

# CHAPTER THIRTEEN

THE USS *Benjamin Franklin* had come into home port in San Diego early that morning.

While taking inventory of the ship's remaining medical supplies, Amelia had mixed feelings on her first deployment coming to an end.

She'd barely seen Cole over the past week. He'd come to the office once, watched her, started to say something, then shaken his head and left. She'd wanted to follow him, to beg him to tell her whatever he'd been about to say, but what good would begging do?

Besides, she wouldn't beg for any man's love.

She couldn't even ask him to help out around the sick ward. Sick call had been slow. The fact they'd soon be home seemed to raise the crews' spirits and few needed their services.

Although she would have welcomed being busy to keep her thoughts from wandering, she also admitted she hadn't been thinking clearly. Probably from lack of sleep and a broken heart.

Why had she let Cole in? Why had she trusted him?

Wasn't that the crux of the matter? Even after the nasty ending to their lovemaking—she refused to call it sex despite him doing so—she didn't regret having made love with Cole, only its less-than-ideal conclusion.

Not that she'd expected claims of undying love and a proposal. Not from Cole.

Which left her wondering what exactly she had expected?

But even as she thought the question, she knew the answer.

She had expected his love.

Because she'd believed he loved her. That's why she hadn't hesitated to make love with him. That as crazy as it had been, he'd fallen in love with her years ago and had come to win her heart.

He'd had her heart from the beginning.

She hadn't known that's what she'd been feeling for him, but she hadn't been able to forget him, hadn't been able to not want him, no matter how much she'd tried.

Which put a dark and gloomy cloud over her future.

If she hadn't been able to forget Cole before, how was she supposed to move on with her life now, after what they'd shared over the past six months?

"You about done?" Suzie asked, crossing to where Amelia worked.

"About."

"I've finished everything I've got to do and plan to go ashore." Suzie eyed her worriedly, placed her hand on Amelia's arm and gave a gentle squeeze. "Call me tonight?"

Amelia hugged her friend goodbye. Who knew when they'd next be assigned to work together, if ever?

"You're going to your parents'?"

A sinking feeling settled into Amelia's stomach. How would she hide her heartache from her parents? They'd take one look at her and demand to know what was wrong.

"I am."

Plus, seeing her parents, being in their home, would envelop her with thoughts of her sister. Of Cole.

She loved him. Right or wrong. Smart or stupid. She loved him.

Who did Cole love? He'd cared enough for Clara to ask her to marry him and spend her life with him. He'd cared enough to keep her secret for two years.

He'd just *used her* for sex. Or to get back at Clara. Or whatever it was he'd done.

She should hate him.

So why didn't she?

It came to her in a blinding flash. Because she didn't believe him.

*She didn't believe him.*

Because he'd not been telling her the truth when he'd said they'd just had sex.

What they shared could never be just sex.

Why hadn't she realized at the time?

Because his words had been poison-tipped arrows and had hit their intended target—her faith in him. But why? Why would he lie to her about how he felt? Because of Clara? Because of his promise to her? She'd confronted her sister and heard the whole story, that Clara had asked Cole not to say anything, wanting freedom and not wanting to face her family's disappointment in her not marrying Cole since they all loved him so much. Clara had feared her father would march her down the aisle and tell her she'd thank him later.

Cole had gone along with her sister's wishes and left, left Amelia when he'd asked *her* to wait for him. Why? If he'd really cared, would he have agreed to just walk away?

Perhaps. If he'd been afraid of his feelings.

Perhaps. If he wasn't sure of how Amelia felt about him, if he wasn't sure if she could ever get past the fact that he'd once been engaged to her sister, if he'd felt as confused as she had.

"What?" Suzie asked, eyeing her oddly. "What?"

"I..." She shook her head, wiped her hands down her pants. "I've got to find Cole."

She needed to ask him why he'd come back that night to her dorm. To ask why he'd arranged his assignment on the USS *Benjamin Franklin*. To ask what he felt for her.

But she knew.

Cole cared for her. He had to. He wouldn't have gone to so much trouble otherwise. Did he love her? Hope bloomed deep in her soul. He just might.

Suzie winced. "That's not going to be as easy as you might think."

"Why not?" *Please, don't let him have already left the ship. Please, no.*

*Please, don't let him have left me again.*

Suzie hesitated, her olive skin wrinkling into a grimace. "He said his goodbyes this morning and was leaving immediately afterwards."

"Said his goodbyes?"

"He came by the dental office." Suzie looked stricken. "He didn't say goodbye to you? Really? He left without saying a word? After, well, everything?"

Amelia's heart shattered. She closed her eyes to hold the millions of pieces inside. Although Suzie didn't know about earlier in the week, she knew some of what had happened between her and Cole.

"Apparently so." Cole had left her. Again. Knowing they might never see each other, that she'd never forgive him for leaving her a second time, he'd left. If he'd really loved her, could he have done that? Could he really have just walked away without seeing her one last time?

Of course he could. Obviously without even a backward glance.

Very simply, she'd been mistaken. Cole hadn't loved her. Maybe he had feelings for her, but not enough. Not nearly enough.

She'd been such a naïve, love-sick fool.

"Oh, honey, I'm so sorry." Suzie wrapped her in another hug. "How could he just leave without saying goodbye? I can't believe he'd do that. I really thought he cared about you."

"Me, too." But they'd both been wrong because if Cole cared he wouldn't have left. Not without saying goodbye. Not knowing how that would devastate her and flash her back to the past.

Back to the first time he'd left her with a broken heart.

"Maybe he had his reasons," Suzie offered.

"I'm sure he did." But none that Amelia would ever want to hear. If she had to cut her heart from her chest, she was finished with Cole Stanley.

Finding Cole and Peyton's room empty didn't surprise her, only confirmed what she hadn't really wanted to believe.

Cole had left her without a word.

Amelia's parents lived a few miles outside the base. Amelia had been surprised her father hadn't come to see her off the ship. Her mother had picked her up from the naval port, claiming the need to stop by the grocery store prior to going home to pick up something for the Admiral, who'd been indisposed at home.

Amelia had wanted to protest, but had decided to be grateful that her mother seemed too distracted to notice her daughter's broken heart. She wanted to be home and curl up in the comfort of the familiar and pretend everything was going to be okay even when she felt as if things would never be okay again.

She knew she was being overly dramatic, that

time healed all wounds. Even ones the size Cole had left in her chest. But right now it was hard to remember that.

"Amelia?"

She glanced toward her mother. The Californian sunshine shone in through the car windows as her mother drove towards the house, casting a glare across Sarah Stockton's face.

"I asked you what was wrong. You don't seem yourself."

Okay, so maybe her mother wasn't that distracted after all.

"It's good to be back on land, that's all." No way did she want to admit to her mother that she'd fallen in love with a man her family would think her crazy for trusting. After all, they had loved and welcomed him up to the point he'd walked away from the eldest Stockton daughter. He'd abandoned them all.

And now he'd abandoned Amelia a second time.

"You're sure? You look distraught."

Amelia nodded, asked about the hospital where her mother worked. Her mother should have retired years ago, but refused to hang up her nurse's cap, saying that as long as there was breath in her body she'd care for the ill.

Amelia was pretty sure her father felt exactly the same way, although apparently he'd gotten more and more wrapped up in military politics over the past few years and spent more and more time in D.C.

"I half expect him to announce we'll be moving, but he may be in for a surprise."

Startled, Amelia glanced toward her mother. "What do you mean?"

"I like San Diego and am tired of being uprooted. I plan to stay here regardless of his career plans."

"You're kidding!" Her mother never balked her father's wishes. Never in the history of mankind. Well, at least never that Amelia was aware of.

"No, dear, I'm not kidding." She reached across the bucket seat, patted Amelia on the knee. "No worries, darling. John won't take a job in Washington if it means leaving me behind."

"He won't?"

"Of course not, dear." Her mother smiled a

knowing smile. "He'd miss me too much to ever do that. Besides, I have my ways of getting him to make the right decisions. Of course..." she winked "...he always thinks he's the one who came up with the right decision and I love him too much to ever point out otherwise."

With that, her mother considered the conversation over and returned her attention to the San Diego traffic.

Amelia stared in awe at the petite dynamo in the driver's seat. All these years she'd thought her mother had simply gone along with her father's wishes. In that moment, she'd seen her mother as the neck steering the head in whatever direction she wanted the Stockton family to go.

"Don't take this the wrong way, because there's no man I admire more, but I always thought Daddy a bit of a dictator."

Her mother laughed. "Are you kidding? Your father is a big pussycat."

"Only you would call Admiral John Stockton a pussycat."

Her mother blushed then laughed a sparkly little laugh that spoke of years of love. "You might be right on that, but he loves you children with all his heart. Perhaps he was a bit stern, but he wanted you to grow into strong individuals. Each of you has."

For the rest of the drive, Amelia was forced to reevaluate every assumption she'd ever made about her parents' marriage. Sure, she'd never doubted her parents' love for each other, but she'd always believed her mother the victim of loving a man who was too militant to fully express that love.

Obviously her mother didn't see it that way. Her mother felt quite loved.

She was still marveling at her misconceptions when they arrived at a typical Californian-style home with stucco walls and a red tile roof. A white sedan sat in the driveway, as did her father's Humvee, his pride and joy.

A few days home would do her good. Amelia loved her family and missed the closeness her siblings and she had shared while growing up. All for one and one for all.

Her mother parked the car, turned off the ignition, jumped out and was grabbing bags of groceries from the backseat before Amelia finished soaking in the fact that she was home. At least, the closest thing she had to home.

If Amelia thought learning her mother led the family just as much as the Admiral did had surprised her, the sight that greeted her when she stepped onto her parents' patio stole ten years of her life.

Her father stood at a grill, flipping burgers, chatting to a man sitting on a wrought-iron swing a few meters away.

The most infuriating, frustrating, unbelievable man Amelia had ever met.

Cole.

Her gaze went back to her father. Why wasn't he screaming at Cole? Threatening to skewer him with a cooking utensil? Instead, he was chatting with him as if they were old buds. Where was the *Twilight Zone* music? Or maybe some camera crew was going to jump out and tell her she was on some hoax show? That she'd been had?

There had to be something, because everything about the scene was wrong.

So wrong she thought she might be physically ill.

Unless Cole had told the Admiral the truth about his and Clara's canceled wedding plans.

Was he seeking her father's forgiveness?

*Had he known she was coming to her parents'?*

Her legs wobbled and she grabbed hold of the frame of the sliding glass doors.

"Amelia?" Her father spotted her. "Don't stand there at attention, girl. Get over here and grab a plate. The burgers are cooked."

Would her legs even hold her up? Could she even put one foot in front of the other?

What was Cole doing at her parents' house?

Could she pretend nothing had happened between them for her parents' sake?

"Hello, Admiral." Just as she'd been doing since she'd been old enough to walk, she saluted the distinguished-looking silver-haired man who, even surprisingly wearing a kiss the cook apron, could never be mistaken for anyone other than a man who commanded authority.

He saluted her back. "Hand me that plate, then tell me all about your deployment, Lieutenant."

She couldn't keep her gaze from going to Cole. "Perhaps you've already heard?"

Her father's expression didn't change. Not that she'd expected it to. None of the Stockton four could ever get so much as an eyebrow rise out of their father. Not that they'd done much to push their father's buttons. High IQs ran in the family and they hadn't wanted to die at a young and tender age.

But even under John Stockton's eagle eye her brain cells all migrated toward Cole.

His blue gaze had settled onto her and she felt heat burning into her skin. He wore civilian clothes. A pair of khaki shorts and a T-shirt that showed off the shape of his chest and narrow waist. How dared he be in her parents' backyard looking so comfortable? So gorgeous? So...like he belonged?

Why hadn't she taken time to stop by the bathroom and wash her face? *Wait a minute.* What she looked like didn't matter. He had left her. Again.

"I asked you to tell me." Her father's shrewd eyes held hers. "Unless there's a reason you'd rather not?"

Her face flushed with embarrassment. Did he know what had transpired between her and Cole? She'd swear her father could see right through her, could read her mind. Hadn't he always been able to?

"No reason, sir," she said all the same, wondering if he'd call her on it.

He didn't, just flipped the burgers one by one onto the plate she held. "Good. Now tell me."

"The deployment was uneventful, sir."

"Uneventful?"

"I worked, learned a lot, got to visit Singapore and made new friends, but you already know all that, sir." *Oh, and I slept with my sister's ex-fiancé who is sitting in your backyard swing listening to every word I say. A man I happen to love and I'm not sure why he is here. Perhaps he came by to give me the opportunity to throttle him for once again breaking my heart?*

"Singapore? I was on board *Kitty Hawk* when she made port call there when the port first opened. But you already know that." Her father's eyes narrowed and again she was struck with the idea that he knew every single thing that had happened between her and Cole. But that was impossible. Cole wouldn't have told her father.

If Cole had, he wouldn't be breathing.

To further confound her, her father took the burger plate from her. "I'm going to take these in to your mother."

He was leaving her outside with Cole? Alone? Had he gone mad?

"I'll go with you."

He frowned. Being frowned at by her father was like being told you'd never eat ice cream again. A very bad thing.

"Or I could stay out here, sir," she amended, barely able to breathe. What was going on? Why had her father just maneuvered her into forced time alone with Cole?

"Good idea, Lieutenant." He nodded, motioning toward where Cole sat in the swing, observing their conversation. "For the record, I said yes."

Yes to what? she wanted to ask, but her father had already disappeared into the house, closing the sliding glass door, and if she didn't know better she'd swear she heard the sound of the lock clicking.

No way would her father, the great Admiral John Stockton, have just locked his middle daughter out of the house with a man her family despised. Or, at least, they had. Apparently things had changed.

"Are you going to say hello?"

Her gaze cut to where Cole had risen from the swing. "Oh, you mean the way you said goodbye?"

Oops. She hadn't meant to say that. She'd meant to be calm, cool and collected. Had meant to act as if it didn't matter that she loved him, had believed he loved her, and he'd walked away from her.

"There was something I needed to do first."

"Something you needed to do before saying goodbye to me? Gee, I see a pattern here."

He nodded, walked toward her. "There were a lot of things that needed to be settled prior to us saying goodbye, Amelia. Surely you realize that."

"Okay, now that we've established that ground-breaking news..." she rolled her eyes, turned away from him because she couldn't bear looking at him a moment longer "...maybe you can tell me something I don't know."

"I love you."

Sure she'd heard wrong, Amelia spun toward him. "What did you say?"

Inhaling a deep breath, he raked his fingers through his hair, and held her gaze. "I love you, Amelia. That's something I'm not sure you know, although you should."

Every cell in her body turned into jumping beans on speed, threatening to burst free and causing complete chaos throughout her nervous system.

"I don't understand." Probably because her brain had turned to short-circuited mush. For a short while she'd believed he cared for her, but even then she hadn't dared to believe he really loved her. She'd hoped, but she'd never quite let herself believe his feelings ran that deep.

"I've been in love with you for years. I'm not sure the exact moment the way I felt about you changed, just that it did." Cole held his breath, watching every play of emotion cross Amelia's beautiful face. She didn't believe him.

Not that he blamed her. Why should she trust a man who she believed had abandoned her twice?

"You're saying you're in love with me?" She sounded ready to burst into laughter.

"I am. I do." He glanced around the backyard, hated it that they had no real privacy, knowing he had to tell her everything, that it was now or never. "Not quite seven months ago, I went to your father and asked for his permission to date you."

Her mouth dropped, her eyes staring at him incredulously. "You did what?"

"I told him that I deeply regretted what happened between Clara and me, but that I couldn't marry your sister. Not when it was you who took my breath away."

Had her eyes grown even wider? "You told him that?"

"And much more," he admitted. "Your father didn't trust me. But he's a fair man, and he did trust you. He arranged for me to be assigned to the USS *Benjamin Franklin*. What happened from there was up to us."

"My father helped you get assigned to my ship?" She picked up the metal spatula, waved it at him.

Hoping she wasn't planning to swat him, Cole nodded. When the Admiral had offered, he'd been floored, but he hadn't had to be asked twice. He'd jumped at the opportunity to spend six months with Amelia, to have six months to work through the feelings they'd once had for each other, that he'd still had for her.

"Let me get this straight. My father helped you sleep with me?"

Cole winced at Amelia's outrage. "That's not how I'd put it."

"How would you put it?" She pointed the tip of the spatula at him. "You were the one who said we were only about sex."

"You and I were never just about sex." He reached for the spatula, but she shook her head, waving the tool menacingly at him. Sighing, he dropped his hands to his sides, wanting to touch her, take her into his arms and tell her all the things in his heart. Could she ever forgive him? "I have never felt about any woman the way I feel about you, Amelia."

Her eyes darkened, closed, reopened with uncertainty in their shiny depths. "Once upon a time you could say the same thing about my sister."

"Clara and I were about friendship and mutual understanding of each other. We got along so well I just assumed the natural next step was marriage because I felt so comfortable with her."

She lowered the grilling tool. "Am I comfortable, too, Cole?"

"Comfortable?" He had to laugh at her question. "Amelia, you are more like a hot poker to my backside."

"Gee, thanks."

"I meant that in the nicest possible way."

"Because hot pokers to backsides have a nice way."

Her sarcasm wasn't lost on him, and he struggled to explain. "You push me to be more, to take chances, to see things in a different light. You make me want to move forward and walk planks that drop off into unknown seas just to experience them with you."

"I don't push you."

"Perhaps you don't realize the effect you have on me, the effect you've always had, but let me assure you, you have impacted my life in untold ways."

"Because I'm Clara's little sister?"

"Because you are you, Amelia Earhart Stockton, the woman I love with all my heart. Let me love you."

Dared Amelia believe him? God, she wanted to. So badly. But to what avail? She could never trust him. Not with her heart. She'd constantly be waiting for the next time he'd leave and wasn't sure she could endure the pain of him abandoning her again.

"You're too late."

He winced, as if she'd struck him with the spatula she held. She dropped the tool onto the grill's side table.

"If you'd said something on the ship, perhaps I could believe you. Perhaps things could have worked. As is, there is too much bad blood between us, Cole."

"Because of Clara?"

"Because of what happened between us," she insisted. "Because of the fact you shut me out, ripped my heart to shreds on the night we made love when you insisted it was just sex, that all we were was sex."

"I had to protect you."

"Protect me? You broke my heart, Cole."

"If I hadn't put space between us, we'd have made love again."

"Had sex, and, yes, you're probably right, we probably would have."

"We might have been caught. I couldn't let you risk your career that way. Not for me. Not when you'd hate me if I cost you your career."

"I loved you, Cole."

"And now you don't?"

She bit her lip, not wanting to answer him.

"Because, like someone once said to me, I don't believe you."

"Don't toss my words back at me. This isn't a game, Cole."

"No, it's not. It's the story of the rest of our life."

Our life. As in singular. He said the words as if they had a life together, as one. They didn't. Did they?

"How can you be sure?" she demanded, tiring of the toll his words were taking on her heart.

He took her hand into his, placed her palm flat over his heart. "That's how I know."

His heart pounded against her palm, beating strong and fast. For her.

"I want to believe you, Cole. I really do."

"I know you do, sweetheart." He put his finger on her chin, tilted her face upwards to his. "Just give me the rest of your life to prove how much I love you."

The rest of her life. What was he saying?

"I asked your father for permission to date you, Amelia. That was six months ago. Earlier today I asked his permission to ask you to be my wife, to do everything within my means to convince you to spend the rest of your life letting me love and take care of you."

Amelia's vision blurred and she was pretty sure

she swayed and that Cole caught her. Either way, his arms wrapped around her, holding her close, keeping her from collapsing onto the concrete patio.

"What did he say?" she croaked, wondering why she wasn't telling Cole there was no way she'd marry him. She didn't want to get married, had never wanted to get married. Except, on the weekend of Clara's wedding, she had wished it was her who'd been going to walk down the aisle to Cole, had wished it was her who'd be spending two weeks with him in a honeymoon suite.

Her father's parting words hit her.

"He said yes," she gasped.

"He said yes," Cole agreed. "But the more important question, Amelia, is what do you say?"

Holding her hand, Cole sank to one knee.

Amelia started shaking her head. "Don't do this, Cole. Please, don't."

He hesitated only a second then, looking up into her eyes, asked her to marry him. "Be my wife, Amelia. My life partner, friend and lover. Be the best part of me and let me spend all my days showing you how much I adore you."

"You adore me?" A crazy question at this point, but his word choice caught her off guard, seemed out of place for a man like Cole.

"I adore you, love you, want you." He squeezed her hand and she realized his trembled. "I need you, Amelia. For two years, I floundered, trying to convince myself I didn't, but I do. I need to know you're there, waiting for me, loving me in return. Maybe asking you to marry me is rushing things, but we've been apart too long already. I know how I feel about you and I know you're what I want for the rest of my life."

"Cole," she began, knowing she had to say no. She didn't want to get married. She didn't want to constantly worry that he'd leave her again someday. She needed her freedom.

But Cole's love was what freed her, gave her the power to be anything she wanted to be. And what she wanted to be more than anything else was his.

Because he was here, loved her, made her whole in a way no one else ever could. Because she'd rather be left by him a thousand times than live a single day without him. Because what she saw in his eyes assured her he'd never leave her, that for the rest of their lives he'd be by her side.

"I love you, Cole."

He pulled her hand to his face, rubbing the back of her fingers across his cheek. "You'll marry me? You trust me?"

Amelia didn't have to think about her answer. She dropped to her knees, cupped Cole's face and nodded. "With all my heart."

# EPILOGUE

COLE smiled at the woman lying in his arms, knowing without doubt he was the happiest man alive.

"What are you thinking about?" Amelia asked, trailing her fingers along his throat, blasting him with a fresh shot of desire.

"What a lucky man your husband is."

"He is, isn't he?" Her lips curved in a delicious, contented smile. She stretched out beside him, contentment and happiness bright in her eyes. "Today was perfect, wasn't it?"

He rose, propping himself on his elbow to look at his wife. She lay against the cream-colored sheet of the San Diego hotel room they'd arranged for their wedding night. In the morning they'd fly out to New Zealand for two weeks of backpacking, kayaking, and just enjoying nature and each other. Not everyone's ideal honeymoon, but when they'd discussed places they wanted to go, exploring New Zealand had topped both of their lists.

"Not anywhere near as perfect as tonight will be," Cole promised. Their wedding had been perfect, but nothing compared to when the world receded and it was just the two of them, together, in love. That was perfection.

"Oh, really?" Amelia's brow arched provocatively, her eyes sparking with challenge. Damn, the woman was going to kill him. But what a way to go. "Because if you expect tonight to top my wedding today, you have your work cut out for you."

"A little hard work never scared me." He bent, nuzzled her neck, teased the lobe of her ear with the tip of his tongue. "I'm up to the challenge."

And would enjoy every moment of meeting that challenge.

"I don't know." She shifted on the bed, arching her naked body beneath the sheet, giving him better access to her throat. "Having the entire Stockton clan home is going to be pretty tough to top."

Topping that would never be an easy feat, but Cole wasn't worried. He had access to Top Secret insider information, such as the sensitive spot at Amelia's nape and the way she liked him to look into her eyes when they made love.

He couldn't get enough of her. The way she'd looked at him when their eyes had met when she'd stepped out of her parents' house to walk between the rows of guests in her parents' backyard. That look had taken his breath away.

Amelia had looked at him as if he was her entire world and Cole knew he'd been looking back at her exactly the same way. She was, and he'd take on the world to keep her safe, to keep her his, to love her all his days.

He breathed in her scent, loving her, wanting her despite them having made love not so long before, knowing she was his forever.

One breath at a time, one kiss at a time, one touch at a time, Cole put everything Amelia into his memory, discovering every nuance of her body, noting every delightful response, relishing her words of pleasure, her cries for more.

Rolling on top of her, Cole clasped their hands,

and smiled down at his wife. "I hope you're enjoying your wedding night so far, Mrs. Stanley."

Amelia stared up at her husband, breathless with need. Did he have any idea what he did to her? How much she wanted and needed him? How happy he made her?

Today truly had been perfect. The California sunshine had been glorious. Her parents' backyard had been transformed into a lush wedding paradise complete with white chairs, white flowers trimmed with navy ribbon, a white lattice backdrop with ribbon and flowers entwined. Having wanted to keep the wedding small, they'd only had about thirty guests, but all the right people had been able to attend. Clara had been her maid of honor. Josie and Suzie bridesmaids. Robert had been Cole's best man, with Peyton and a schoolfriend of Cole's serving as groomsmen. Sarah Stockton had been a gorgeous mother of the bride and the Admiral had looked handsome decked out in his uniform as he'd given Amelia to Cole.

And Cole. No man had ever looked more gorgeous in his uniform. No man had ever given so much to a woman.

Not hiding the emotion rushing through her, Amelia held Cole's gaze, loving the feel of his body over hers, loving the adoration in his eyes.

"Just so long as you're mine..." she squeezed his hands, enthralled by the strength of his fingers laced with hers, of the strength in everything about this wonderful man "...every night is perfect, Cole."

"I'm always yours, Amelia. My heart, my love, all that I am I give to you and you alone. Forever."

And as he kissed her, made love to her, Amelia knew Cole's promise was true. Her husband was a man of his word.

## MILLS & BOON PUBLISH EIGHT LARGE PRINT TITLES A MONTH. THESE ARE THE TITLES FOR APRIL 2011.

NAIVE BRIDE, DEFIANT WIFE
Lynne Graham

NICOLO: THE POWERFUL SICILIAN
Sandra Marton

STRANDED, SEDUCED...PREGNANT
Kim Lawrence

SHOCK: ONE-NIGHT HEIR
Melanie Milburne

MISTLETOE AND THE LOST STILETTO
Liz Fielding

ANGEL OF SMOKY HOLLOW
Barbara McMahon

CHRISTMAS AT CANDLEBARK FARM
Michelle Douglas

RESCUED BY HIS CHRISTMAS ANGEL
Cara Colter

MILLS
BOON